Double Delights

Kit Kyndall

Published by Amourisa Press, 2016.

Join Kit's Mailing List[1] **to receive notification of new releases and access bonus chapters for your favorite books. You get six free books just for signing up. If you prefer to receive notifications for just one, or a few, of Kit's pen names, you'll have the option to select which lists to subscribe to at signup.**

---

1. http://kittunstall.com/newsletter/

Double Delights

Kit Kyndall

Blurb

WHAT'S WORSE THAN LOSING your fiancé? Having him break the news two weeks before the wedding during dinner with his family. Tamsyn is shamed by the way Will handles things, but so grateful when his identical brothers step in to take care of her.

It turns out Dean and Evan want to do more than care for the curvy beauty. The men share everything, and Tamsyn is just the wife they want. If she's brave enough to explore the option, she might find they are exactly what she needs.

This contains naughty bits that should only be read by adults.

A Peek Inside:

"MY MOUTH IS ON FIRE." She licked her lips, wincing at the slight tingle remaining from the spice. "How do you two stand that heat level?"

"We like it hot."

She glanced at him from the corner of her eye, certain she had detected a hint of smokiness in his reply. "But my mouth—"

Dean sighed, suddenly turning to face her. "Let me show you how to cool it down."

Before Tamsyn could ask more, his lips slanted over hers in a firm kiss. She almost jerked back in shock, but her second impulse urged her closer. Her mouth tingled in a new way now as his tongue licked her lips, lightly coaxing them to part at the seam. She moaned when his tongue swept inside her mouth to flirt with hers.

She had no idea where the kiss might have led if the sound of the door opening hadn't made her jump away from him like a scalded cat. Her heart raced in her ears, and she stared at him with wide eyes, uncertain how to feel or what to think. To her surprise, and his, she said, "That didn't really cool me off."

His lips twitched. "Yeah, me neither. Go get your ice cream and see if that helps."

She was happy to have the excuse to flee and got to her feet to join Evan in the kitchen. He had already unpacked two cartons of ice cream, along with several toppings. Tamsyn kept her gaze on the dessert and bowls, feeling the flush of guilt turning her cheeks hot and making it impossible to look at him. Why did she feel guilty for kissing his brother?

The obvious answer was she was just a few days out from a broken engagement to their brother, and she should feel ashamed for having kissed anyone so soon after the relationship ended. There was an element of truth to that reasoning, but she knew it wasn't the whole truth.

There was a more personal part too, as though she had betrayed Evan by kissing Dean. Was it because she saw them as a unit, and she felt like she had been wrong to kiss just one? She had no idea, but knew she felt unbalanced or something.

She helped Evan serve the ice cream without saying much. He was frowning by the time they'd finished scooping vanilla and chocolate in the bowls, before covering it all with strawberry sauce and chopped nuts. He held the whipped cream can and adorned each sundae with a curl of cream.

"How's your mouth?"

Her eyes widened. Had he somehow guessed? "Uh..."

"Here, this should help cool it down." He brought the nozzle of the can to her mouth.

On autopilot, she opened up so he could spray a shot inside. A gob filled her mouth, and she swallowed quickly.

"Oops, missed some." He pointed to the corner of her mouth. "Let me." His tone had deepened.

She watched, mesmerized, as Evan bent down while he nudged her chin upward. It didn't even occur to her try to evade his mouth as it settled on hers. His lips were firm, yet soft, stroking against hers in a teasing way before his tongue flicked out to lick the cream from the corner of her mouth.

DOUBLE DELIGHTS

Chapter One

THE GAINES' DINNER table was loud and boisterous, as usual. As a teenager, when she had befriended Jaely after the family had moved next door, it had taken Tamsyn a bit of time to adjust to everyone always talking at once when she had joined the family for the occasional dinner. After ten years of being friends with Jaely and fourteen months with her brother Will, three as his fiancée, she couldn't imagine their dining room any other way.

It now felt strange on the few occasions when she shared a meal with her parents, who were often busy and not home. The Wallace family was quiet and well-mannered, ever mindful of the rules of decorum. It boggled her mind to imagine Father and Mother sitting down with the Gaines clan for a meal. They had interacted throughout the years in an aloof way, but the two groups didn't mix socially.

They would have to at the wedding, which reminded her to ask her best friend, "Did you find out if the candles for the centerpieces come in snow?"

Jaely shook her head. "No, the clerk told me the closest they have is white smoke."

Tamsyn couldn't hide a frown. "I really wanted snow. It has to coordinate with the rest of the linen."

"You aren't likely to get snow in July," said Dean with a saucy wink.

"Smoke is a possibility," added Evan. "I hear there are some wildfires still burning in the mountains."

Jaely rolled her eyes. "Could you two please be serious?"

Tamsyn giggled. "I don't think they've been serious from the day they were born." She gave the twins a fond smile. They were five years older than her, but they certainly didn't seem a lot more mature or distant. She had counted them as friends from the day she'd met them, along with the other Gaines children, ten years ago. Back then, she'd been chubby, knock-kneed, and wearing braces. Jaely and Will had been in a similar boat, but the oldest identical Gaines boys had already outgrown that awkward phase.

Her cheeks burned as she suddenly recalled the fierce crush she'd had on the twin boys back then. Feeling guilty for the thought, she turned back to her fiancé, who looked pale. Sweat beaded his lip. With concern, she leaned closer to him to ask softly, "Are you feeling all right, Will?"

He nodded jerkily, but didn't reply.

After looking at him for a moment, puzzled when he wouldn't meet her gaze, she turned back to Jaely with a shrug. "I suppose white smoke will have to do."

"That reminds me, love," said Flora, the matriarch of the Gaines family, "Lacey's dress is finished. The dressmaker has us down for one last fitting a few days before the wedding, to make sure there are no last-minute alterations, but everything is ready."

Tamsyn smiled at the smallest Gaines, and Lacey's nose wrinkled as she grinned in return. "Are you still ready to be my flower girl?"

"Yes, Tamsyn." The four-year-old squirmed in her delight. "Me can't wait."

"*I* can't wait," corrected Conrad, earning a puzzled look from his tiny daughter.

"How come you's excited too, Daddy? You can't be a flower girl."

Tamsyn joined in with the giggles around the table until she realized Will looked queasy. Touching his arm, she said, "Are you ill? Do you need a doctor?"

"I can't..." He struggled to breathe, tugging at his collar.

"Is it an allergy to something?" asked Flora, the second to pick up on her son's distress. "There aren't any allergies in the family, but I read just the other day that you can develop an allergy to something that never seemed to bother you before. Isn't that fascinating?"

Ignoring her future mother-in-law's babbling, as Flora was apt to do, she asked, "What's wrong?"

"I can't do this." He said it with an explosion of sound, as though the words had burst from him via cannon.

"What?"

Will gulped audibly as the table fell silent. "I just can't, Tamsyn."

She frowned. "Can't what?"

"I can't go through with this. I can't marry you."

She blinked, too stunned to react for a second. "What? Is this a joke?" Will rarely indulged in pranks, and she couldn't imagine he would think this was funny, but that had to be what he was doing. Nothing else made sense.

Will bunched up his napkin and set it on the table. "No joke, I'm afraid." He sighed, looking heartbroken. "I just don't love you the way I'm s'posed to, Tamsyn." Will's copper eyes, so much like his father's and siblings', were moist with suppressed tears. "I thought I did, but then..."

She shook her head, clutching her own napkin like a lifeline. "This...it makes no sense...I... You can't really be calling off the wedding?" And like this, at the family dinner table? She burned with mortification and the first stirrings of anger.

His shoulders sagged, as though he bore the weight of all the heavy glares directed toward him in a physical manner. "I met someone else at my work. She makes me feel things I didn't even know I could." Still looking like the victim, he reached out to pat her hand. "I'm very sorry that I didn't say something sooner, Tamsyn. If I had met her just a week earlier, I wouldn't have proposed—"

She jerked her hand from his, having to fist it to resist the urge to slap him. "You met her a week after we got engaged?" At his sheepish nod, she reeled back in her seat, suddenly desperate to be away from him. He wasn't the man she knew, or thought she had known. "How could you do this? Why didn't you say something sooner?"

"I didn't want to hurt you."

"Fine job you did of that," said Dean, his contempt for his brother obvious in his tone and sparking copper eyes.

"This isn't your business," said Will.

"You made it our business when you chose to humiliate Tamsyn this way, in front of all of us," snarled Evan.

"I can't handle this." Will shoved away from the table, glaring at his brothers before turning awkwardly toward Tamsyn. "We'll talk later, okay?"

"Talk?" She stared down at her clenched fists, shrugging him off when he tried to touch her shoulder. Talking to him held no appeal. Right then, she wanted to be as far away from him as possible.

Her head was whirling as she stood up, and she stumbled, but tried to keep walking. Nausea burned a trail up her throat, and she cringed as she tried to imagine telling her parents what had transpired. They would no doubt be not-so-secretly thrilled, having made no effort to hide their disapproval of Will and his unorthodox family. It hurt her heart to imagine dealing with them, knowing how they would react.

Strong arms caught her as she started to fall, and she looked up into Dean's face, idly wondering how anyone could confuse him with his twin, even though they both wore their overly long russet locks in a similar style. The minute differences in the shape of their eyebrows and his slightly fuller lower lip made them easy to tell apart.

Evan was suddenly there on her other side, providing support with an arm around her waist. Their solid bodies provided protection for her curvy frame and kept her from falling. Tears scalded her eyes and burst free with a hoarse sob.

"Do you want to go home?" asked Evan.

She shook her head, unable to imagine confiding anything to her parents yet. She wished now she had gotten her own place after graduation and starting her new job, but it had seemed silly when she and Will had plans to marry soon, and he already owned his own house.

"Do you want to stay here?" asked Dean, looking uncertainly at his parents and Jaely, who had cornered Will to keep him from leaving.

"Too much..." She whimpered, leaning even more on the two men, as pain coursed through her. It wasn't physical pain, but she felt the emotional sting everywhere.

"Right." Dean and Evan shared a look before he said, "You're coming home with us."

She didn't argue. She couldn't think about anything at that moment except escaping from Will's presence. Tamsyn let the two men lead her from the house of her second family. The family that had almost been hers in an official capacity. Ragged sobs tore from her aching chest, and she collapsed against Evan in the back seat as Dean drove them.

LATER, SHE DIDN'T RECALL the drive to their apartment in the center of downtown. She didn't remember getting out of the car or walking between the twins, though she assumed she must have. Her next clear memory was of sitting on one of the large sectional sofas in their spacious living room, grasping a cup of hot coffee she had yet to sip, and staring mindlessly at the pristine white wall. "Snow," she whispered.

"What, sweetie?" asked Dean, who sat on her left. Evan had sprawled on her right.

"Your walls. They're snow-colored, like the candles I wanted for the centerpieces..." She trailed off, another quiet sob escaping her raw throat. Tamsyn knew she must have been crying for a long time, but she had remained unaware of it beyond a visceral level. The pain in her throat let her know she hadn't been silent.

Dean pulled her more firmly against him, so her head rested on his chest. Evan scooted closer, putting his head on her shoulder, his hand rubbing small circles on her thigh.

"Why didn't I see it?" she rasped. Had she missed something? Tamsyn searched her memories, looking for signs. "He was kind of withdrawn, but I really thought it was just from planning the wedding. He never said...never seemed..." She bit her lip, recalling something that had concerned her at the time, but she had forced herself not to dwell on it, thinking it would resolve itself. "He said we were boring. We never did anything new, and I didn't seem interested. I just lay there, and I never initiated sex." She closed her eyes. "He must have been comparing me to her."

Dean grasped her hand, squeezing gently. "Will is acting like an idiot, Tamsyn."

"Definitely." Evan rubbed his cheek against her shoulder. "If he's giving you up, he's nuts."

"Everyone's going to know." Her voice broke, and sobs rose in her again. "Everyone will know I'm a failure. I wasn't good enough. Not slim enough or adventurous enough in bed. I couldn't be what he needed..." The next sob choked her, but she was aware enough of Evan moving away, leaving her bereft. Not that she could blame him, with the way she was carrying on.

Tamsyn didn't resist when Dean pulled her into his arms, with her lying across his lap. His hands were soothing on her back, and even in her hazy state, she inhaled his crisp male scent with appreciation. He didn't hide it beneath pricy cologne the way Will did.

For some reason, that made her cry harder, and it took her a few minutes to realize Evan was back, sitting next to her. When she managed to lift her head from Dean's chest, she eyed the glass of water and small blue pill he held out to her doubtfully. "What's that?"

"A mild sedative. Do you remember that I used to sleepwalk?" At her nod, he said, "I don't much anymore, but if I've gone wandering more than a night or two in a row, I take these for a few nights to reset my sleep pattern, and no more sleepwalking." Evan smiled. "It's safe, I promise."

She held out her shaking hand, but he shook his head.

"Open up."

It was oddly intimate to have him put the pill on her tongue, and a jolt of something shot through her when his fingers brushed the inside of her mouth as he withdrew. She obediently sipped the water he held and swallowed the sedative. Tamsyn was too drained to argue and too unstable at the moment to care that she was seeking chemical refuge. It was only temporary, and she would still have to deal with everything when it wore off. There was no harm in a small reprieve.

She groaned, her throat flaring with pain at the sound. "Going to have to cancel everything," she said hoarsely. "Flowers, dresses, reservations." Tears streamed from her eyes again, though she should have been dehydrated by now. "The honeymoon." She had been looking forward to their trip to the Caribbean ever since the night he'd proposed.

Evan sat beside her again, leaving her half on Dean's lap as he settled her legs across his. "It will be okay. We'll handle everything."

"By that, we mean we'll let Jaely and Mom handle everything," said Dean with a small grin. "We don't know enough of the details, but they will."

"I guess I should be glad he finally told me two weeks before the wedding instead of leaving me at the altar alone." The mental image seared into her mind, sending a fresh wave of shame through her. "How am I going to face everyone?"

"Don't worry about it for now." Evan started rubbing her bare legs in a motion that was probably supposed to be soothing, but was actually leaving her feeling a little...breathless.

"How can I not worry? It's so embarrassing."

"You'll have to face everyone at some point, but for now, you're going to stay here with us." Dean spoke firmly, as though the matter was decided. "We'll hide out here, ignore the phone, and eat takeaway—god knows I wouldn't subject you to our cooking. You've suffered enough."

She gave him an anemic smile. "I really can't though. My job—"

Evan arched a brow. "You're what, the junior secretary to the assistant's dog walker? They can do without you."

She scowled. "I'm in admin support."

Dean arched a brow. "What do you do?"

She flushed. "Everything all the people above me tell me to do," she admitted with a sigh. "It turns out my parents may have been right about the degree in Renaissance art."

"Useless," said Evan with a sigh. "That's okay. We're filthy rich, so we'll take care of you until you're back on your feet."

She swiped her cheeks. "I'm not sick or dying, Evan. I've just been dumped."

"Don't argue with us," said Dean with mock sternness. "You know you want to stay here."

"I really shouldn't…"

"We have chocolate," said Evan.

"And champagne," added Dean.

"And a huge jetted tub in the room you'll use." Evan danced his fingers around her ankle.

"Free video games," said Dean.

"I do love your games," she admitted.

"Excellent. We have one we just wrapped up that will need testers. You can be our first."

She was starting to feel woozy, but managed to nod. "I'd love to." Tamsyn thought about pointing out that she might not be in the best state of mind to help detect bugs in their software, with her thoughts so preoccupied, but a yawn stole the words.

"Okay, let's get you to bed, love," said Dean.

She tried to stand on her own, but they wouldn't let her. She let out a yelp of surprise when Evan lifted her into his arms to carry her. With a sigh of contentment, she ignored the voice telling her to insist that she walk on her own and just enjoyed the experience.

No man had ever carried her before. She hadn't permitted it from fear of being too heavy, but she didn't think she was too much for Evan's broad shoulders and tall frame. She was completely confident he could support her curves, and that he wanted to do so.

She held on reflexively for a moment when he eased her onto the bed, but forced her hands to let go. Tamsyn snuggled into the soft pillow as someone placed a blanket over her.

"Should we try to wake her up to undress?" asked one of the twins.

"No, I don't think we can. That stuff knocks you out fast." That had to be Evan, since he sounded like he had experience with the medication.

"Maybe we should undress her?"

Tamsyn felt a dart of alarm—and something else—shoot through her at Dean's suggestion, but couldn't open her eyes or manage to form a protest.

Evan groaned. "That would be some serious temptation, Dean. I think it's best to just let her sleep in her shorts and shirt for now."

"Maybe her bra?"

Tamsyn was slipping into unconsciousness, but she swore she heard both men groan as though in pain. Sweet relief in the form of blackness swept over her before she could be sure or hear more of their discussion.

Chapter Two

TAMSYN AWOKE WITH A dry mouth, burning eyes, sore throat, and pounding head. It was a bit like a hangover, without the fun of the night before. With a stifled moan, she sat up and stretched, groaning again.

Reluctantly, she forced her eyes to open fully and blinked at the first sight of the room where the twins had left her. This was a guestroom? Wow. The bed was huge, as was the room, and the furnishings tasteful, though clearly expensive. The white walls and gray carpeting were similar to what they had in their living room, and she wondered if they had carried the theme throughout the high-rise apartment.

Her bladder urged her to abandon her visual exploration in favor of finding the bathroom. She didn't take much time to notice her surroundings until she sat on the commode. As she did her business, Tamsyn eyed the marble bathroom with wonder. That was indeed a huge tub. The black marble, swirled with gold and accentuated by gold taps, sank into the floor at least three feet deep.

Unable to resist the lure, she stripped off her clothes, dropping the bra and panties on the counter to wear them again when she left the apartment. After her bath, she intended to slip on the forest green terry robe on the door, deciding it was modest enough for wearing around their home.

The tub filled faster than she would have expected, laced with the scent of vanilla oil she had poured in at the beginning. She walked down the stairs and sank into the water, finding purchase on the bench built into the side. Even seated on that, the bathwater came up to her neck. She was of average height, but it was that deep.

Perhaps they had such a deep tub because they were both so tall. She knew Evan and Dean had to be close to six-five. Will wasn't short, by any means, but the twins still towered over him.

Thinking of Will made her chest ache, and her eyes burned again. Desperately, she cast her mind for some kind of distraction as she flipped on the jets. For some strange reason, her imagination provided her an image of the twins in the tub. She frowned, deciding that was silly. They wouldn't bathe together.

But they might be in the spacious bathtub with a woman. Did they share women? She'd wondered that a few times when she was younger, somewhere between her awkward teenage crush phase and before she started dating Will. They seemed to do everything else together, so did they make love to a woman as a pair? What would they do to that lucky lady?

Her eyes popped open when she realized she had been thinking some seriously naughty thoughts about two of her oldest friends. It was doubly inappropriate since the only reason she was here was because their little brother had broken up with her so cruelly.

She shook her head, marveling at the strange reactions and thoughts grief could prompt. Normally, she wouldn't have even considered such things, having outgrown that infatuation long ago. It was just a desperate attempt to keep herself from mourning her broken engagement and facing the humiliating consequences. She knew there would be pity and sympathy to her face, but could just imagine the kind of vicious speculation that would take place behind her back.

It would only be worse if and when Will made his relationship public with his other woman. There would be a few kind souls who might believe Will had been a jerk, but there would be many more wondering what was wrong with Tamsyn that she couldn't keep her man? Was it as simple as she was voluptuous and curvier than the accepted standards of modern beauty, or were there other reasons? Was she a nag? Sexually inhibited? Seriously kinky? People would talk and wonder, stare and whisper. She shuddered with dread at the prospect.

In an effort to block out the thoughts, she slipped off the bench and plunged under the water. Her dark hair spilled out in a fan around her head when she looked up through the water. She stayed there until she couldn't hold her breath any longer, breaking the surface with a clearer head.

There wasn't anything she could do about the gossip, but for now she was safe in Dean and Evan's apartment. It was cowardly, not to mention a great imposition on their friendship, but she had no intention of leaving just yet. She was still too emotionally bruised to face anyone else. Even the prospect of seeing Jaely didn't cheer her, since her friend would want to conduct a postmortem and try to figure out what went wrong. Then she'd be full of ideas about how to fix it and get Will back.

That should have been the course she wanted to pursue. Tamsyn should have been eager to brainstorm with her best friend. Instead, she wanted to avoid the whole fiasco. What did that say about her relationship with Will? Was she too angry to even consider reconciling for now, or did she really want to end things? Had he done her a favor, albeit in a horribly awkward way?

She shook her head, sending droplets of water flying. It was too soon to decide how she felt about anything. She was still too blindingly angry with her former fiancé to strategize or decide her next course of action. All she wanted to do was hide and avoid the world for a bit.

As she slipped from the bath and dried off, she couldn't help a small smile that spread across her face. Her hideaway came with a matching set of caring hunks. There couldn't be much better scenarios in a situation like this. Of course, it would have been better if they weren't related to Will.

The terry robe was soft and fluffy. She belted it tightly around her waist, deciding it would certainly preserve her modesty. The robe touched her ankles and rose almost to her ears. She turned sideways to inhale deeply, trying to place the elusive scent clinging to it. There was detergent, but something else underneath that had to be from Evan or Dean. One, or both, of the twins had worn the garment. For some reason, that thought sent a shiver down her spine.

She forced away all silly thoughts as she left the bedroom. As soon as she opened the door, the scent of coffee lured her down the hallway, and she padded through the thick carpet with her bare feet. It was only when she entered the kitchen to find both men seated at the square table that the disconcerting realization that she wasn't wearing underwear around them caught up with her. Stifling a mingled gasp and shocked giggle, she hovered uncertainly in the doorway.

Evan saw her first, giving her a cheery grin. "Morning, sweetie. Hungry?"

Her stomach growled, and she shrugged. "I guess I am."

"There're pancakes and sausage," said Dean, pointing to the plates on the table.

She narrowed her eyes at the food as she walked over to the counter to brew herself a cup of coffee with their single-serving machine. "I thought you promised not to cook for me."

He laughed easily. "Don't worry, love. The sausage was frozen, and the pancakes come from a box."

"Processed food will kill you," she said with a hint of disapproval before taking her mug from the machine.

"Not as fast as our cooking," said Evan.

She sipped the rich brew appreciatively. "This is good coffee." Even better than her parents' preferred brand, which they bought at some coffee specialty shop in the trendy part of town.

"It should be. Comes from Africa, and each plant is given its own growing attendant, paid fair-trade certified wages. It's nurtured in the shade via organic methods and hand-harvested by pygmies, because they can reach the beans easier without bruising the plant."

She rolled her eyes. "You're so full of it, Dean." Her lip quirked as she imagined her parents would probably actively seek out such a product and brag about it to their friends—in a subtle way, of course. It wouldn't do to be indiscreet about their wealth.

Evan chuckled. "It comes from Whole Foods. It is organic and shade-grown, but I don't think personal attendants or pygmies were involved in any way."

"If they were, I hope the pygmies got fair-trade wages too." She sat at the table, taking the plate Dean offered before selecting some of the morning offerings. When her pancakes were piled with chopped bananas and pecans, and she had three sausage links, deciding she had earned a small indulgence, she dug in. "This is surprisingly good," she admitted a short time later.

"Worth every last minute it will shave off our lives," said Evan, finishing his last bite.

"Tomorrow morning, we'll have to have bacon," said Dean.

She groaned. "You're trying to kill me before I have to face everyone, aren't you?"

He tilted his head as though considering. "I think I heard a slice of bacon will kill you nine minutes sooner, so you'd have to eat a lot of bacon in the next few days."

She sighed. "That's okay. I love bacon, but I'm not suicidal."

"Good." Evan squeezed her shoulder as he walked by her to put his plate in the dishwasher. "Will isn't worth that kind of melodrama."

Tamsyn managed a small smile. "It happens that I agree with you. I have no intention of being dramatic. The Wallace family would die of shock and shame if I carried on in public." Her smile fled as she remembered the way she'd reacted yesterday. "If my parents had seen me go to pieces like I did all over you guys, they would have spoken harshly and reminded me to behave with decorum."

"No offense, but your folks are a total cliché, love." Dean drained his coffee. "They're pretentious and high-brow."

"They nearly died when your family moved in," she admitted, recalling their aghast reactions upon learning their elderly neighbor had left her large home to her great-nephew, who had an even larger family.

Evan chuckled. "We must have been a shock for the entire neighborhood, running around and laughing."

"You dared behave like children...well, mostly Jaely and Will." She stuttered a bit over his name, finding it hurt.

"That's a lousy thing to say," Dean said. "You're implying we weren't childlike?"

She snorted. "Immature isn't the same as childlike, my dear."

"Are you implying we didn't grow up?" Evan looked wounded, but the twitch of his lips gave him away.

"I'm not implying anything," she said overly sweetly. "Stating it straight out..."

"If you aren't careful, you'll be treading into tickle territory," said Evan with a hint of warning.

"We haven't had a good tickle war in ages." Dean looked morose.

She held up her hands, pretending to shudder. "Not that." On more than one occasion over the years, she had ended up being on the losing side of tickle wars, pinned to the floor as the twins had tickled her mercilessly, while she giggled and gasped, trying to beg for mercy.

"Darn." Evan sounded crestfallen. "I guess we'll have to find something else to do."

Her eyes widened as her mind jumped somewhere it shouldn't. Ruthlessly, she cut off the inappropriate thought. "You mentioned a new video game I could try?"

"Come on, Tamsyn." Dean got up from the table and took her arm to pull her up. "Let's go introduce you to *Legend of Klutz*."

Moments later, she was curled up on the couch with a large-screen laptop on her lap, delving into their newest comedy/fantasy game. It crossed her mind that she was supposed to meet with the bakery in thirty minutes, but found the prospect of playing video games much more enjoyable than handling the details of her wedding. Again, she wondered what that said about her relationship with Will as she focused on the story of the clumsy knight set on rescuing the dragon from the princess, who wanted to turn the poor creature into a new cloak and boots.

THE NEXT FEW DAYS PASSED in a similar manner. She would take a dip in the tub upon waking, join the men for breakfast, play games before lunch, and then spend the afternoon talking or watching movies, always sprawled on the couch between Dean and Evan.

It was getting harder and harder to avoid facing all the people who would know by now that she had lost her fiancé. It was also getting harder to remember why she had been so upset about losing him. Mostly, it was getting insanely difficult not to notice she was in the constant company of two sexy men who seemed determined to make her the sole focus of their attention. She knew they were just being kind and doing their utmost to distract her from the heartbreak Will had inflicted, but she wasn't always able to keep it firmly in her mind that she was only their friend.

They had spent the day battling it out on the console system, though they hadn't played any of the Gaines' games. "It would be an unfair advantage," Dean had said with an angelic air when she asked why they weren't playing any of their designs. Afterward, they had ordered in Thai food that was too spicy.

"It was delicious, but I really want ice cream," she said with a mock whine a little while after they'd eaten.

"Evan'll be back soon, love," said Dean. They were lying on the floor amid a pile of throw pillows to watch cheesy '80s movies.

"My mouth is on fire." She licked her lips, wincing at the slight tingle remaining from the spice. "How do you two stand that heat level?"

"We like it hot."

She glanced at him from the corner of her eye, certain she had detected a hint of smokiness in his reply. "But my mouth—"

Dean sighed, suddenly turning to face her. "Let me show you how to cool it down."

Before Tamsyn could ask more, his lips slanted over hers in a firm kiss. She almost jerked back in shock, but her second impulse urged her closer. Her mouth tingled in a new way now as his tongue licked her lips, lightly coaxing them to part at the seam. She moaned when his tongue swept inside her mouth to flirt with hers.

She had no idea where the kiss might have led if the sound of the door opening hadn't made her jump away from him like a scalded cat. Her heart raced in her ears, and she stared at him with wide eyes, uncertain how to feel or what to think. To her surprise, and his, she said, "That didn't really cool me off."

His lips twitched. "Yeah, me neither. Go get your ice cream and see if that helps."

She was happy to have the excuse to flee and got to her feet to join Evan in the kitchen. He had already unpacked two cartons of ice cream, along with several toppings. Tamsyn kept her gaze on the dessert and bowls, feeling the flush of guilt turning her cheeks hot and making it impossible to look at him. Why did she feel guilty for kissing his brother?

The obvious answer was she was just a few days out from a broken engagement to their brother, and she should feel ashamed for having kissed anyone so soon after the relationship ended. There was an element of truth to that reasoning, but she knew it wasn't the whole truth.

There was a more personal part too, as though she had betrayed Evan by kissing Dean. Was it because she saw them as a unit, and she felt like she had been wrong to kiss just one? She had no idea, but knew she felt unbalanced or something.

She helped Evan serve the ice cream without saying much. He was frowning by the time they'd finished scooping vanilla and chocolate in the bowls, before covering it all with strawberry sauce and chopped nuts.

He held the whipped cream can and adorned each sundae with a curl of cream.

"How's your mouth?"

Her eyes widened. Had he somehow guessed? "Uh…"

"Here, this should help cool it down." He brought the nozzle of the can to her mouth.

On autopilot, she opened up so he could spray a shot inside. A gob filled her mouth, and she swallowed quickly.

"Oops, missed some." He pointed to the corner of her mouth. "Let me." His tone had deepened.

She watched, mesmerized, as Evan bent down while he nudged her chin upward. It didn't even occur to her try to evade his mouth as it settled on hers. His lips were firm, yet soft, stroking against hers in a teasing way before his tongue flicked out to lick the cream from the corner of her mouth.

When he stepped back, grabbing his and Dean's bowls as though nothing had happened, she picked up hers and followed him numbly from the kitchen. Her mind was awhirl with confusion as she tried to make sense of having kissed two men—two brothers, and the brothers of her ex-fiancé—less than ten minutes apart.

What was she thinking? What was she doing? As she took her place on the floor between them, studiously avoiding meeting either set of eyes, she stared at her ice cream and tried to rationalize her behavior. There was no reasonable explanation for acting in such a way, and she realized she had to leave before things got really awkward. She squirmed with shame as she imagined one or the other mentioning their casual kiss in passing to the other twin. As soon as they talked, they would know she was a slut.

"If you stare any harder at that ice cream, you're going to melt it with that sour look." Dean licked his spoon thoroughly before scooping up another bite.

"Why are you so dour?" asked Evan.

"Dour?" Dean rolled his eyes. "What is she, that butler on that Abbey show?"

"*Downton Abbey*," said Tamsyn distractedly. "Carson."

"Yeah, him."

She bit her lip, not sure how to answer. Instead, she forced herself to take a bite of the ice cream, though the sweetness tasted almost bitter on her tongue, especially when she remembered how each of the men beside her had tasted. The same, yet different enough that she could tell them apart.

"What's on your mind?" asked Evan.

"I think it's time I went home." It took a lot of courage to say that, mainly because she wasn't ready to face anyone so far. She hadn't even talked to her parents yet, though her mother had called her twice on her cell phone before she'd turned it off. What she wanted was to stay in the safe little cocoon they had created for her until they grew sick of her and made her leave. If she hadn't screwed up everything by kissing both of them, maybe that would have been an option, at least for a bit longer. Now, she had no choice but to leave.

"No way," said Dean, sounding firm. "We caught you fair and square."

"We're keeping you," said Evan after he licked his spoon.

She rolled her eyes, not able to summon a smile. "You two are cute, but it's time for me to—"

"Finish your ice cream." Dean sounded a bit grumpy. "Watch *The Breakfast Club* and forget about this leaving stuff."

"You don't understand." She bit her lip again, certain there must be a groove worn from her teeth by now. "I have to."

"Why? Didn't you say your boss had already left a message that if you didn't come in this morning, you were fired?" asked Evan.

She nodded, not feeling a twinge of regret that she would no longer be an admin slave at the company where she had worked. "It's not that."

"Your parents are worried?" suggested Dean.

"Probably, but not that either."

Dean sighed. "It's because I kissed you, isn't it? I shouldn't have done that."

"You kissed her? I think you mean I kissed her," said Evan.

She cringed, expecting an argument to explode, and both of them to turn to her with harsh names and harsher accusations.

"Did you really? I thought we were going to wait," said Dean. "Give her time to get over Will and be ready for more."

Her eyes widened, but she didn't get a chance to speak.

"Yeah, that's true. So why did you kiss her then?" Evan tilted his head as though awaiting his twin's reply with mild interest.

Neither of them sounded upset, and as their words sank in, she slowly lifted her head, realizing they had talked about both of them kissing her. About giving her time and waiting until she was ready for more. More what? What did they want from her? "I don't understand." She frowned. "Aren't you disgusted that I kissed both of you?"

"No," said Dean, sounding so unconcerned that it seemed impossible he was lying.

Evan nudged her with his shoulder. "Of course not."

Tamsyn shook her head, thoroughly confused. "What do you want from me?"

Dean and Evan shared a long look before Dean said, "I think it would be easier to go back a bit and explain us."

She nodded, taking a bite of her ice cream automatically as her gaze remained glued to Dean's face, watching his lips form syllables.

"I don't think you can truly appreciate how it is to be a twin, especially identical, unless you are one." Dean set aside his mostly finished bowl so he could stretch out on his side, elbow bent so his hand could brace his head. "In many ways, it's like being two halves of a whole."

"I'm the better looking half, of course," said Evan as he scooted around to lie in front of Tamsyn, allowing her to easily switch her gaze between both of them.

She rolled her eyes, but didn't agree or disagree, not wanting Dean to get sidetracked from his explanation.

"Evan and I tried splitting up and pursuing individual interests. We even lived apart for a while during college, if you remember?" At her nod, he continued. "The problem was our interests are basically the same. We had the same hobbies, same friends, and same—"

"Taste in women," said Evan as he licked his spoon.

"It felt like there was a piece missing when we were apart."

Evan held up his hand. "Lest you be confused, it's not some tragic story where we can't be parted. We can stand the separation, and a few hours or days isn't a big deal. We're just always aware that something is absent."

"That makes sense." She ate a bite of ice cream, self-consciously aware of their eyes watching every movement of her mouth as she licked the spoon.

"When our first game was a hit, we bought this place and moved in together. We were still dating other women at the time, separately." Evan sighed. "It just never worked out."

"The women couldn't stand feeling like our brother was more important than they were, so dating went nowhere besides short-term."

"Until Ezra." Evan said the name with a happy sigh.

Dean chuckled with a strong hint of fondness. "Ezra opened our eyes."

"Who was he?" she asked.

"She. She was the first woman who wanted to date both of us at the same time. Ezra wasn't jealous of the time we spent together, because she understood being part of a unit."

Tamsyn didn't like the burning feeling in her chest. She shied away from labeling it, having a feeling it was a close cousin of jealousy. "How?"

"She was an identical twin too. Had been anyway," said Evan. "Her sister had died in a car accident a few years before. Until then, Ezra and Evelyn shared a husband."

"Oh." She wanted to ask how that had worked, from the legalities to the practicalities, but didn't. "What happened? Did he leave her after her sister died?"

"No, he died with Evelyn."

Though her chest still burned with that unlabeled emotion, she also felt a swell of pity. "That poor girl."

"It was hard for her, but I'd like to think we helped make things easier for a while," said Dean.

"Why isn't she still around?" she asked, probing carefully.

"We weren't completely compatible. It happens in the best relationships that sometimes, the differences are too vast. Ezra moved on, and so did we—this time with a clear understanding of what we wanted, and what would work for us," said Dean.

"And what is that?" Why was it so hard to ask that question?

"We knew we wanted to share a woman, and that we wanted one who didn't feel threatened by our closeness, who could understand she was an integral part of the relationship and not get jealous of our bond." Evan said it casually, as though he hadn't just listed some very difficult-to-find factors.

Her mind was reeling with questions and thoughts. Tentatively, she asked, "Er, have you found that?"

"Sometimes, but not anything long-term. There's been no woman we've been with long enough to introduce to our family."

At Dean's words, she tried to imagine Flora and Conrad's reaction to their sons' girlfriend, but couldn't picture it. Shaking her head, she asked, "What does this have to do with me?" But she had a fairly good idea and had to admit her first reaction wasn't outrage. Instead, it was curiosity.

"It's not like we've been sitting around pining for you," said Evan.

"But we've been interested for a long time."

"Since you're twenty-first birthday." Evan leaned closer, so he could trail his fingers down her hand.

She frowned, trying to remember what might have sparked their interest. "I don't really—"

"Remember?" asked Dean with a laugh. "You were smashed, love."

"You probably don't remember dancing with us—"

"Both of us at the same time." Dean grinned. "You were the filling in our Oreo, and you were very uninhibited."

Her face burned with embarrassment, but she truly couldn't remember the dance. She didn't doubt them, but the lack of memory bothered her. "What else did we do?"

"Oh, nothing. It was just a dance. A very intimate dance," said Evan, his tone smoky.

"Somewhere between you rubbing against both of us and your eventual falling asleep on the couch, we realized we wanted you," added Dean.

Evan sighed. "Of course we didn't tell you."

Her mouth dropped open. "But why?"

They shared another look, one that seemed full of interest, as though she had given them something to discuss in-depth. "For one, you're younger than us, so we figured you probably didn't have much experience. Dating two guys might freak you out."

"And deciding to let one of us have you, and the other be without, wasn't happening," said Evan.

"We decided to be noble and step aside." Dean scowled. "And a few months later, Will stepped in. If we'd had any idea how that would turn out—"

"We would have told you that night how we felt."

"The next morning," said Dean with a small chuckle. "You were too drunk to remember anything we might have said that night."

She flushed, recalling how inebriated she'd gotten. It had been her first experience with alcohol, and she hadn't realized at that point she was such a lightweight. Two years later, she knew not to have more than two drinks if she wanted to remain coherent and standing. "What does...dating you both entail?"

"The usual," said Evan.

"Just your standard leather, whips, chains—"

"Floggers and handcuffs—"

She huffed. "Will you two stop being so immature? Just for a moment," she hastened to add, not wanting them to think she wasn't happy with their personalities. "I need details so I can think...decide."

"We can start with something simple," said Evan.

"How about dinner tomorrow night?" asked Dean.

"I..." She bit her lip, unsure how to proceed. "It's only been a few days since Will dumped me."

"If you aren't ready, that's fine," said Dean. "We don't want to push you."

"Even if you decide you don't want to date us—and we realize it's a lot for any woman to consider—we'll still be your friend." Evan squeezed her hand gently.

"Always that," added Dean firmly.

Unless they did meet a woman who was perfect for both of them, and she didn't like knowing Tamsyn had once been considered for her role. The men would have to respect their wife's wishes. The thought of some other woman sharing the twins made her stomach roil with nausea, and she had to bite back the instinctive urge to protest. If she couldn't even think rationally about them dating someone else, how would she ever cope with the reality?

The timing had been wrong before, but she suddenly saw a new opportunity that she didn't want to deny herself. Her childhood crush was gone, though her attraction lingered. There was a chance to have something special with them if she could let go of convention and embrace the opportunity.

Licking her lips, she said, "Dinner would be nice." She expected a wave of nerves, or some apprehension, but calmness swept over her instead. As they settled back in their places, returning to the movie, she found the peacefulness remained even though she couldn't shut down her brain.

Because of her upbringing, Tamsyn was rather traditional in many ways. She had certainly never imagined dating two men at the same time, especially in these circumstances. When she'd had the crush on the twins, she had been unable to envision choosing between them, which had helped her get over the infatuation and focus solely on the friendship. Now, she realized why. As a younger girl, she hadn't been able to intuit what she could as an adult. She hadn't understood fully why she couldn't separate them, but now she did.

Dean and Evan were a pair. Neither would be whole without the other, and it made perfect sense that they would want one woman to share. Her only anxiety was if she could actually be that woman? She didn't think attraction would be an issue, because they had plenty of that. For her, the issues that would be problematic would all involve the social side. She couldn't imagine her parents accepting such a relationship. Many of her friends wouldn't understand either. Would Jaely and her parents be tolerant?

With a sigh, she vowed to stop worrying about the potential problems and focus just on taking it slowly. Their date might be a disaster, forcing them to return to strictly friend status. There was no reason to worry about future events unless and until they reached that point.

Chapter Three

WHEN TAMSYN RETURNED to her parents' home the next day via taxi to retrieve evening wear for her dinner date with Evan and Dean, she was surprised to find her mother in the sitting room, having tea alone. Usually, she would have been at one of her myriad social commitments or visiting with her friends at the country club. She couldn't refuse when Diane said, "Join me," in that firm tone that brooked no argument.

Feeling reluctance she tried to hide, she accepted the tea her mother offered and made no effort to break the silence. She sipped the bitter brew served without milk or honey, hid a grimace, and waited.

"Why have you not returned my calls, Tamsyn?"

She put the tea on the table near her stiff chair. "I'm sorry, Mother, but I haven't felt like talking to anyone."

"Well, you might have had the courtesy to let me know yourself that your engagement had ended, rather than leaving the task to that woman." Diane sniffed.

That woman must be Flora, because Jaely was often dubbed her "unsuitable friend." Sympathy for Flora had her twisting her hands in her lap, and she made a mental note to thank the other woman for performing the unpleasant task. "As I said, I haven't felt up to discussions."

Diane sniffed again. "At least you're here now. There are many tasks with which you can assist me."

She frowned. "Like what?"

"There are gifts to return, and you'll have to write apology notes to everyone—"

"Apology notes?" She fisted her hands in her lap. "I'm supposed to apologize for my fiancé dumping me two weeks before the wedding, so he could be with another woman?"

Diane lifted a shoulder. "My dear, etiquette demands you recognize the inconvenience your invited guests have endured. I do realize the circumstances aren't your fault." She sniffed again. "However, if you had chosen more wisely, as we begged you to do, perhaps you wouldn't have ended up with that juvenile oaf."

She gritted her teeth, struggling not to say anything rude. "I'm afraid I won't be able to offer any assistance. I simply came to get some clothes."

Diane sniffed again.

"Mother, do you need a tissue?" she bit out, earning a glower from the older woman. "In that case, I shall leave you."

"Why do you need clothes? Where are you staying?"

She skipped over answering the latter half of her mother's inquiry. "I have a dinner date tonight." She experienced an unexpected lightening sensation at the confession.

Diane's eyes narrowed. "I suppose this means you'll be getting back with him?" She sighed dramatically. "It does save me a great deal of work. I held off on sending out notice of the canceled wedding, assuming you would end up crawling back to William."

Her lips twitched, and she felt naughty when she said, "Go ahead and send the notices, Mother. My date isn't with Will."

Her mother scowled. "It's unseemly to be dating a new man just days after your broken engagement."

"Don't worry, Mother. I'm not having dinner with a man." She couldn't help a small grin, and a spark of rebellion, when she added, "It's two." Without waiting for a response from her mother, she stood up and left the sitting room, heading toward her bedroom.

She had retrieved a suitcase and several outfits by the time her mother walked in without even a knock. Tamsyn didn't look up at her as she continued retrieving underthings from the drawer.

"I know this has been difficult for you."

The hint of understanding in her mother's voice made her look up with surprise. "Um, yes, it has."

A moment later, any sign of sympathy faded, and her lips pursed. "That's no excuse to make tasteless jokes. I assume that was your hilarious way of informing me you've been staying with that pair of reprobates."

With a small sigh, she resumed packing, not looking at her mother again. "Dean and Evan kindly offered me a place to hide for the past few days."

"How long will you remain in hiding? You can't expect me to bear the brunt of your humiliation. People are gossiping."

Tamsyn stomped to the wardrobe to take out several garment bags, not bothering to sort through them in her annoyance. "People will always gossip, Mother, but I don't particularly care right now. I need time, space, and understanding."

"That's all very well at home, but you have to make a public appearance. You must face people and show them you are still strong. We'll do dinner tonight at the country club. Rudolph will be home in a couple of hours. There is plenty of time to get ready."

"No."

"Don't be silly." Diane glanced at her watch. "We even have time to nip by the salon."

"No," said Tamsyn again. "I already told you that I have a date tonight."

Diane sniffed. "Dinner with your...friends can certainly be postponed."

"So I can have dinner with yours and prove I'm not shattered? After all, we wouldn't want anyone to think you'd raised me improperly." Tamsyn didn't hide her scowl as she lifted her case and the garment bags. "I'm not canceling my date."

"It's hardly a date—"

"But it is." She gave her mother a small smile, relishing the look of shock that bloomed on her pinched features after Tamsyn said, "I'm having a dinner date with Dean and Evan, and I am considering dating both of them. I've already kissed both of them."

Her mother paled. "That's outrageous."

"Hmm." She walked toward the door, waiting for her mother to move.

"You're lying."

"Am I?"

Diane's eyes narrowed. "If you're going to carry on like a harlot, I won't acknowledge you."

"Harlot...that's a word you don't hear every day." Tamsyn couldn't decide if her aloof amusement was genuine or just a good façade. Either way, she was enjoying riling her mother.

"I'm serious." Diane put a hand on the door. "If you leave my home with the intent of becoming a whore for two men, you won't be welcomed back."

"I love you, Mother." As her mom blinked, she didn't allow Diane to say anything. "I love you and Father both, but I'm tired of trying to live up to what you think is right and be the person you're trying to force me to be. I've never been good about conforming to your world, but I have sincerely tried. I can't do it anymore." She softened her voice. "Surely you don't expect me to give up a chance at finding happiness because the arrangement is unorthodox?"

"I expect you to behave like a lady, as you were raised to be." Diane's purple-blue eyes, so much like Tamsyn's own, burned with disgust she made no attempt to hide. "I haven't wasted twenty-three years of my life to have you turn out this way."

Sadness curbed the hint of dark glee she'd been feeling from outraging her mother. Shaking her head, Tamsyn reached for the doorknob and pulled lightly. Her mother immediately dropped her hand. "I'm sorry you feel like you've wasted your time on me." She didn't look back as she slipped through the doorway and walked down the stairs.

Diane's footsteps followed her, though the other woman didn't speak again until Tamsyn opened the front door. "I mean it, and you know Rudolph will support me on this. If you leave now, to go to them, don't even think about coming back."

"I won't." With a calming deep breath, Tamsyn stepped over the threshold of her parents' house without the certainty of knowing she would be back. It made her chest ache to think about not having her parents in her life, but she had to live her life in a way that would make it worthwhile.

She kept a straight back and proud demeanor as she walked to her car, still parked in front of their house as she had left it several days ago. It wasn't until she had stowed everything inside and driven a few blocks away that her hands started shaking. A deep breath turned into a ragged sob, and she pulled over, uncaring of the person standing on their lawn watching her with interest.

She took a tissue from the box on the console and dabbed her eyes, determined not to have another crying jag after so many recently. Tamsyn breathed deeply until her sense of calm was restored. Once under control, she merged back onto the road and continued driving.

Questions and doubts swirled in her head, primarily among them what would she do now? Dating Evan and Dean was a strange and unfamiliar new adventure, but it was only dating. That didn't mean she could live at their house indefinitely. Now that she had walked out of her parents', she was stumped on where she would go. She couldn't impose on the twins much longer.

If only she hadn't put so much of her savings into the wedding. Her parents had been recalcitrant about financing, since they had disliked her choice of grooms. Will had put in some, but she knew most of his savings had gone to the down payment on the house they were meant to share after the wedding.

Jaely lived with two other girls, and there was no space for a guest, even temporarily. She certainly couldn't ask Will to stay at his place, and the idea of asking Flora and Conrad to borrow a room for a while was too humiliating to consider. She was sure they would welcome her, but it would be too awkward.

It wasn't just her savings. Her stomach churned when she remembered her recent return to unemployment. No one would rent her an apartment without a job, even if she could scrape up a couple thousand dollars for the deposit and rent.

Panic was twirling merrily inside her by the time she parked in the guest space the garage attendant had directed her toward and emerged from her car. She cast an appraising gaze at it, deciding she could probably sell the sensible hatchback gifted to her by her parents after college graduation. That should give her living expenses until she found a job. When she found employment, she'd just have to take public transportation, like many of her fellow Seattlites. She had traveled via public transport before and could do so again.

Feeling a little better with a small plan in mind, she took her belongings into the elevator and up to their floor. When she knocked, Dean opened the door a moment later, his hair rumpled as though he'd been running his hands through it continuously.

"Good afternoon. Whatever you're selling, we're buying." He winked at her before taking her hand to pull her inside. Then he called, "She's home," over his shoulder.

She got a pleasant little shiver from hearing him refer to the apartment as home, even though she knew he meant in the context of it being his home. Tamsyn didn't protest when he took her suitcase. A second later, Evan joined them in the foyer and grabbed her garment bags.

"This is a lot of stuff for one date," said Evan with a chuckle.

She squirmed, remembering how she had told them she was going home to get a dress for dinner. "Uh, well, things changed while I was there."

As they entered the guestroom she was using, Dean dropped her case on the bed, and Evan hung the dresses in the huge walk-in closet, barely filling a tiny portion of the available space.

She sank onto her bed, not surprised when Dean and Evan sprawled out beside her.

"What happened, love?" asked Dean.

"My mother expected me to apologize to my guests for getting jilted."

Evan whistled. "That's harsh."

"Yeah. Not only that, she had issues with me going on a date so soon after the broken engagement." She couldn't suppress a giggle. "If you'd seen my mother's face when I told her I was dating two men, not one, you would have died laughing."

"You told her?" Dean asked, looking impressed.

"Ballsy." Evan squeezed her knee.

"Except she didn't take it well and told me I'd be disowned if I continued on my path to harlotude with the reprobate pair. That's you guys."

Dean arched a brow. "Harlotude?"

"Is that a word?" Evan grinned.

Tamsyn managed a small smile of her own. "Of course she phrased it properly, but harlotude fits." Her smile disappeared. "She considers me a whore for even considering dating two men."

"Your parents have sticks wedged so firmly up their asses..." Dean trailed off.

She arched a brow. "Can you honestly say we won't face a similar reaction from everyone we know?"

Evan shrugged. "If we get to the point of announcing our relationship, I imagine we'll get some nasty looks and ugly words, but who cares? The only opinion that matters is ours, don't you think?"

She bit her lip. "I want to be like that, Evan, but my upbringing... You have no idea how guilty I feel sometimes just using a dinner fork for my salad *and* entrée."

Dean laughed. "We'll buy you an entire set of silver to rival the Queen Mum's if that will assuage your guilt."

She rolled her eyes. "Yeah, silverware will do the trick." Tamsyn leaned back against the pillow, and they joined her a moment later, Dean's head on her stomach, and Evan's on her shoulder. Her fingers insisted on stroking the red-brown strands that were already so disheveled, as her other hand grasped Evan's at her side. "I want to be brave."

"Then be brave." Evan squeezed her hand. "Or don't, and we'll fight your battles for you."

She mock-shuddered. "I've seen what Sir Klutz did. I don't know if I'd trust you two in any battles."

"We'd always fight for you," said Dean, with an unusual hint of seriousness.

"Absolutely." Evan brought her hand to his mouth to kiss her fingers. "I guess the question is if you want to fight for us?"

Tamsyn turned her head to meet his copper gaze. "Yeah, I do." She had no doubt about that, despite all her other fears and worries. "Now get out of here so I can make myself presentable for our dinner date."

THEY PICKED HER UP at her door right at seven p.m., to ensure they would arrive in time for the eight p.m. reservation at Palisade. She caught her breath at the sight of them standing on her "doorstep." The twins both wore charcoal gray jackets and slacks. Dean wore a hunter green silk shirt, and Evan had opted for sapphire. They made her mouth water, and she had the greedy urge to drag them into her room. It was a bit like having unlimited access to the candy shop, and she wanted to sample everything.

"You look exquisite," said Evan, his gaze raking her from head to toe in the red sheath she wore that emphasized her hourglass figure, eyes pausing at the dusting of sequins across the low bodice that swept up the left shoulder. Her right shoulder was bare, and the dress stopped a couple of inches above her knees. Crimson heels displayed her legs to best advantage, though they pinched her toes.

"Good enough to eat," said Dean.

She grinned. "I was just thinking something similar about both of you, but I don't want to ruin my appetite." Grasping her evening bag more securely, she stepped out of the guestroom and entwined her arms with one of each of theirs. "I've never been to Palisade."

Dean look surprised. "Really? It's iconic. How can you call yourself a Seattlite if you haven't eaten there?"

Tamsyn giggled. "My budget doesn't allow for Palisade, and my parents have always eschewed it, because they are disdainful of its appeal to the masses. They might have to dine with anyone who can afford it."

"Even a couple of loser video game designers?" Evan tisked his tongue. "No wonder they steered clear all these years. It's scandalous the riffraff that place lets in."

The drive to the restaurant was filled with playful banter, but even her amusement couldn't completely silence the faint buzz of nerves. Her blood seemed effervescent, and she was excited to see where the evening would lead.

Palisade was as elegant as she had expected, and she had no issue with the possibility that *nouveau riche* might be contaminating the atmosphere. The *maître d'* led them to the patio, and she walked to the rail, wrapped with lights, to look at the water. Multiple sailboats moored in the marina spread out around the restaurant, with the open waters of

Elliott Bay serving as a backdrop. A light breeze ruffled her hair, but it was pleasant.

After a moment, she turned to the table where the *maître d'* waited, holding her chair. She sat down as Dean and Evan took seats on either side of her at the round table. As soon as the employee left them, their server appeared to take their drink and appetizer orders.

As they waited for their cocktails and ocean tower sampler, she leaned closer to them, finding it comforting when they scooted their chairs closer to press against either side of her. A small shiver went through her, though she wasn't sure if it was the brisk breeze that blew around them or the proximity of the twins. "This is lovely." Trying to avoid sounding—or feeling—jealous, she asked, "Is this where you usually bring your first dates?"

Dean's lips quirked. "Not at all. We've brought Mom and Jaely before, but those are the only other women we've been here with."

"It's certainly designed to make an impression." She leaned back slightly as their waiter reappeared, placing a Lavender Cosmo in front of her before serving Dean his Thai Basil Gimlet and offering Evan a glass of sparkling mineral water. Waiting until after he'd taken their orders and left, she waved at his glass. "Don't you drink?"

He shrugged. "Sometimes, but it makes my sleepwalking worse if I drink too much. Plus, I'm the designated driver this evening." He winked. "You can have one for me."

She smiled. "Not if you want me to walk out of this restaurant. Two is my absolute limit, and I'm saving my second for a glass of wine with dinner."

"We could carry you out," said Dean, leering.

Tamsyn rolled her eyes. "You'd have to, and then you'd have to put me in bed and let me sleep it off. I'm useless after more than two."

"Useless? I remember you being quite...adventurous." Evan trailed his fingers down her wrist. "That dance—"

"It's one of my favorite memories." Dean took her other hand, bringing it to his lips to kiss her fingers. "Maybe we can recreate it sometime, without all the alcohol to rob your memory."

Tamsyn accidentally locked eyes with an older woman two tables away. Her lips had pursed in disapproval, and she made a point of staring at the way the twins were both touching her with familiarity before wrinkling her nose and looking away.

Self-consciousness assailed her, and she had to resist the urge to tug her hands free. Reminding herself that she didn't care what that judgmental old hag thought, but cared very much about not hurting Dean or Evan, she returned her attention to her dining companions.

Their appetizer arrived, and she didn't think of refusing when Dean offered her an oyster. She took it delicately from the shell, deliberately flicking her tongue against his fingertips as she swallowed the perfectly seasoned shellfish. She moaned with delight at the explosion of flavor on her tongue as Dean licked his own fingers.

"My turn," said Evan.

Tamsyn opened her mouth, expecting another oyster or a prawn, and breaking into giggles as Evan extended a lobster tail on a fork. Shaking her head, she pushed his hand away lightly, saying with affection, "Idiot."

He looked hurt. "What? I can't feed you too?" His eyes gleamed with amusement though.

"Infantile." Dean tisked his tongue. "I keep telling him to grow up."

"Please don't. I like you both this way. It's…comfortable."

Evan looked askance. "We're comfortable?"

"Terrific. We're like sweatpants after work." Dean looked wounded.

"Or your favorite pair of old shoes."

"I could walk all over you," she said with a hint of teasing which morphed to a touch of discomfort when Evan's expression turned serious.

"You could. You can do anything you want to us, Tamsyn."

Unprepared for his intensity, and certain he wasn't referring to sexual things—or just sexual things—she distracted herself by taking a prawn and brushing it against his lips. "Open up."

Evan took it obediently, but sighed. "No lobster tail for me?" he asked after he'd swallowed the oyster.

"You'll have to feed that to yourself."

"Spoilsport."

They worked their way through the appetizer at a leisurely pace, sometimes feeding each other bits of ahi poke or prawns, since the oysters were eaten first. They had just finished the last of the ocean salad and lobster when their server came with their entrees and wine.

Tamsyn enjoyed her scallops, but found she preferred Evan's risotto, while Dean kept wanting to trade his creamed spinach for bites of her farro. Eating with them was fun and sensual. Their presence seemed to enhance the taste and aroma of all the dishes. The light brush of their breath against her cheek as they took turns offering her bites from their own forks seemed to enhance the visual appeal of the food.

She was practically in a food coma, though her body also sang with unreleased sexual tension, by the time their server brought dessert. They had opted to share the trio of crème brûlée. After a couple of bites of each, she said, "I can't decide if I like the lemon or the vanilla bean better. The dark chocolate is delicious, but too rich."

"We'll help you decide." Dean took a dollop of the vanilla bean brûlée and touched it to his lips. "Try the vanilla again."

Tamsyn's stomach clenched as she leaned forward to meet his mouth. Taking her time, pretending to appraise the brûlée, she thoroughly licked the dessert from his lips before dipping her tongue between them to taste him quickly. When she pulled back, she licked her lips. "Yum."

"Lemon?" Evan had already added brûlée to his lips.

Tamsyn repeated the process with his mouth. When she pulled away, she put her chin on her hand. "I just can't decide. Who could pick between such perfection?"

"There's no need to pick." Evan dabbed his mouth with his napkin, probably to remove the trace of stickiness from the brûlée.

"You can have both, and all you want."

She was warm all over, and hot at her core. Her panties were damp, and she was impatient to get back to their apartment, assuming they would make love to her tonight. It should have alarmed her a little, since she had never had sex with anyone on the first date, but as she had told them, they were familiar and comfortable. Not that she expected the sex to be tranquil. It was going to be explosive.

Tamsyn excused herself to go to the restroom as they settled the check. The ladies' room was just as posh as the rest of the restaurant, and if she hadn't been eager to get back to her men, she would have sat on the black velvet couch that beckoned, to see if it was as cushy as it looked.

She had just touched up her lipstick when another stall opened. A woman around her age in a silver dress came up to the sink beside her, shooting her an appraising look. Tamsyn realized she had also been seated on the patio, at the same table as the disapproving woman. Looking quickly away, she tucked her lipstick back in the bag and started to leave.

"Excuse me?"

Stifling a sigh, she said, "Yes?"

"May I ask you a question?"

Certain it was to do with the twins, Tamsyn braced herself for a rude comment that probably wouldn't be a question, except maybe along the lines of: How can you be so amoral? "What is it?"

"Those men you're with...the twins..." Her cheeks took on a touch of pink. "You're with both of them, right?"

Tamsyn nodded just once.

"Lucky you." She grinned. "Um, I wanted to ask you if they're the guys who own that video game company?"

Tamsyn blinked, taking a moment to process the other woman's words. She had expected her to ask about how they were in bed, since she didn't seem disgusted by the unorthodox date. "Yes, they are."

"I thought I recognized them from an article in *Seattle Entrepreneur*." Looking a bit embarrassed, she said, "Would you be able to give them my card? I'd love to beta their new designs."

Tamsyn's lips twitched, but she suppressed a smile and took the card carefully. "I'd be happy to." Since the woman had taken her dating the two in stride, she would be sure the guys definitely got the card and gave her the opportunity to play their games, if possible.

Buoyed by the other woman's surprising reaction, she returned to the table. Dean and Evan rose as she approached, Dean holding out her wrap. She walked beside them from the restaurant, starting to turn toward the parking lot when Evan caught her arm gently.

"Let's take a walk."

Even though the tips of her shoes pinched her toes, she didn't protest. Who would say no to a moonlit walk along the marina with two handsome men in tow? The strolled down the line of boats for several minutes, holding hands. She tossed back her head, letting the wind rifle through her hair until it had mostly destroyed the loose topknot she'd fastened.

"Here we are."

She stopped when they did, turning to look at a sailing yacht. "What's this?" Even as she asked the question, she saw the name on the boat. "*Gemini*? Is this yours?"

"It is. Forty-five feet of sailing bliss," said Evan.

They led her up the ramp, holding her carefully as she stepped onto the deck. Tamsyn clung to their arms with her hands as the waves churned lazily under the vessel, making it sway. Once she was accustomed to the motion, which was barely detectable standing onboard, she let go of their arms.

"The grand tour," said Dean, taking her hand again. He led her around the main deck, showing her the controls and the bathing platform, with Evan trailing behind.

When he led her below, her nerves stretched taut as she expected seduction to commence. "No sailing tonight?" she asked as she eyed the luxurious main area, where the kitchen, dining area, and living room formed an open space. There were four doors leading off the main living space.

Dean shook his head. "Someone has to be on the deck at all times when sailing, and we want to spend our time with you. We'll take you out tomorrow, if you want. We just thought we'd stop by and show you *Gemini* since we're in the area."

"And make sure you like sailing," said Evan. "I thought I heard somewhere that you get awful seasickness."

Tamsyn lifted a shoulder. "I haven't been since I was fifteen. Last time was with one of my parents' friends." She grimaced, recalling how she had feigned nausea to escape the inappropriate leering and attempts at touching from her dad's business contact. When she had later told her parents the truth about why she'd insisted on going back to shore, they had seemed more annoyed with her than with the pervert. "My last experience made me sick, but I'm willing to try again." She didn't think any touching or advances that would take place with Dean and Evan would fall into the inappropriate category. More like welcome and eagerly sought.

To her surprise, they didn't stay long on the yacht, and other than showing her the three sleeping cabins and the two heads hidden behind the doors, they didn't make any attempt to get her close to a bed. After planning a trip tomorrow, they left the yacht and walked back to their coupe.

Her nerves seem to tauten as they drove back to the apartment, and she was preparing herself for the forthcoming experience. Tamsyn wanted both of them very much, but she wasn't sure how the threesome thing actually worked. Would they want to be inside her at the same time? Considering she had never enjoyed anal, that could be problematic.

Tamsyn had worked herself into such a state of nervousness by the time they reached the apartment and walked inside that she didn't notice they had led her back to her guestroom. She clenched her fingers and took a deep breath, wanting to enjoy making love with Dean and Evan, not be lost in uncertainty.

First Evan, and then Dean, gave her a passionate kiss at her door. Her pinched toes, along with the rest of her, were tingling by the time she'd had both of their mouths, and she blinked as Dean stepped back, slowly disengaging her hand from his hunter green shirt. "What…?"

"You kissed her senseless," said Evan with a chuckle.

"It was a joint effort." Dean made a show of false modesty.

Tamsyn blinked again. "Er, don't you want to…come in?"

"Sure, but that wouldn't be right."

Evan shook his head. "It's too soon."

"We want more than a quick fuck, Tamsyn." Dean cupped her cheek.

"There's no rush." Evan caressed her bare shoulder before pressing a light kiss to the skin that made her shiver with delight. "I might change my mind if you wear this dress again though."

Feeling a bit off-kilter, she managed a flippant, "I'll be sleeping in it."

He groaned. "She's wicked, brother."

Dean laughed. "Good would be so boring."

To her consternation, tinged with just a bit of relief, they left her at her door and strolled off to the other side of the apartment.

Dean paused at the end of the hallway. "The date's over. Would you like to watch a movie or something?" He wagged his finger. "Something innocent?"

She laughed. "You two have probably never been innocent. I think I'll pass tonight. I'm tired and want to be well-rested for our cruise tomorrow." It was only after she had closed the door and leaned against it that Tamsyn admitted she was far more disappointed than relieved about their gentlemanly behavior. With a small, disgruntled sigh, she went to the bathroom to strip off the dress and prepare for bed.

Her blood was still racing in her veins, and she skipped nightwear to slip between the cool satin sheets wearing just her skin. She was hot and aching, wishing Dean and Evan hadn't been so sweet and insistent on taking things slowly. Their thoughtfulness was going to be the death of her, she decided, as she turned over for the fourth time in a futile attempt to get comfortable and fall asleep.

Chapter Four

THE DAY WAS GLORIOUSLY sunny and hotter than usual for July in Seattle, making it a perfect day for sailing. They returned to the *Gemini* with a full hamper and other necessities for a day on the water. Evan and Dean had them out of the marina and into Elliott Bay in no time. The gentle swaying of the boat didn't bother her as they moved north toward the San Juan Islands.

A crisp breeze made her appreciate the long-sleeve wrap she wore over her bikini, and she gratefully accepted the cup of coffee Dean held out to her about twenty minutes into their sail.

"It'll warm up a bit as it gets later. When we drop anchor for a while, that will reduce the wind." His gaze dipped to the modest bit of cleavage her cover-up revealed. "We'll have you out of that thing sometime today."

She rolled her eyes and waved him back to the controls with his brother, content to stand at the side, leaning on the rail of the seat that doubled as the bathing deck—not that they would need that today. It was much too cold for the average swimmer to jump into the Strait of Juan de Fuca without a wetsuit.

The sun was bright, making her feel more cheerful than she had for days. It had been nice to retreat to their apartment and hide away for a little while, but she was ready to get back into the sunshine and on with her life.

Within two hours, they had reached the islands, and the twins chose to drop anchor off the shore of one of the uninhabited islands. Tamsyn made herself useful by helping Evan spread the tablecloth on the deck so Dean could unload the hamper. She sat down between them, watching the growing spread of food with a growling stomach. The bagel and cream cheese she'd had earlier had left no lasting impression, especially when faced with the mound of delicacies.

The wind had lessened dramatically with the yacht stopping, and she watched with appreciation as the men stripped off their T-shirts, leaving them both wearing lightweight cargo pants. Feeling the need to tease in turn, she unbuttoned her cover-up and draped it on the pile with their shirts, leaving her in a white bikini top and purple checked gingham capris over her bikini shorts.

"Heaven," said Dean, his gaze glued to the generous swell of cleavage spilling from her bikini top.

"It is a perfect day," she agreed with a demure smile.

"Perfect," echoed Evan as he offered her a blini topped with caviar and a dollop of sour cream.

Slowly, she took the treat into her mouth, licking the tips of his fingers seductively. "Delicious," she said with her mouth full, pushing aside the twinge of guilt at the bad manners. How she wished she could banish Diane's voice of motherly guilt to a faraway place and never hear it again.

"We know how you feel about forks—" Dean offered her a strawberry with his fingers.

"So we left them behind," finished Evan as he popped the cork on a bottle of champagne. The foamy beverage splashed out, hitting her on the chest. "Oops," he said with a marked lack of sincerity.

She rolled her eyes. "Subtle, dear."

"Quite." Dean leaned forward to lick a trail of champagne from her neck and across her collarbone. His mouth hovered near the edge of her bikini, but he withdrew before exploring the flesh underneath the fabric.

With a small sigh of frustration, she accepted the glass Evan extended, taking another bite from the plump strawberry along with a small sip. Tamsyn closed her eyes in pleasure. She didn't open them again until more food brushed her lips. Warily, she opened her eyes to find Dean offering her a chunk of grilled chicken on a skewer in a perfectly mature manner. It wouldn't surprise her to find a chicken leg stuffed in her mouth with either of their quirky senses of humor.

They nibbled their way through the various delicacies procured from some mysterious source, and Tamsyn enjoyed being the center of their attention. She might have expected it to be awkward, or feel like she had to evenly divide her attention between them to avoid hurt feelings, but being with them in this context felt as normal as the interactions they had shared before dating.

"Time for dessert," said Evan, wielding a can of whipped cream.

Recalling what had happened the last time he had cream, she licked her lips. The can came closer to her mouth, but he detoured at the last moment to spray a line down her chest.

"You're going to get her sticky." Dean clicked his tongue. "Let's take care of that."

She sat frozen as he unsnapped the strap holding the bikini top around her neck. It fell to the deck with a whisper of sound completely drowned out by the gentle slap of the ocean against the yacht's bow.

"You have amazing breasts, love," said Evan.

She didn't resist when he pushed her down on the tablecloth. The deck was hard against her back, but she soon forgot about her discomfort when the twins knelt on either side of her. The cream was cold on her nipples when Evan dotted them, and she shivered with a mix of anticipation and the chill.

"My favorite—berries and cream." Dean emphasized his point by trailing his tongue around the plump contour of her nipple.

"Sweet." Evan's mouth engulfed her nipple, swiping away the cream with one stroke of his tongue before he began sucking her sensitive bud.

"Mmm." Dean continued his slower exploration, teasing her as he removed the cream with delicate strokes of his tongue.

Tamsyn writhed under the dual attention, her body aching with desire. She had never felt this way before, and the contrasting ways they touched her only enhanced her pleasure and further increased her need.

She reached for both of them, placing a hand on each of their biceps. Caught up in the magic of their mouths, she couldn't manage to do more than squeeze the flesh under her hands before stroking them with her fingertips.

Evan was the first to venture lower, his mouth moving down the soft roundness of her tummy, pausing to blow gently into her belly button. She squirmed and giggled, but the gaiety fled when he reached the waistband of her capris.

Feeling shy, she froze when his fingers breached the elastic. She didn't want him to stop, but she couldn't completely block out the voice in the back of her mind calling her a fat whore. It was no surprise it sounded just like her mother.

Dean had finally removed the rest of the cream from her nipple and moved his mouth upward. His gaze locked with hers, the warm copper shining with concern. "You okay, Tamsyn?"

After a brief hesitation, she nodded. "I'm just nervous. Being naked for the first time in front of you guys..." She trailed off.

He arched a brow. "You aren't actually naked yet."

"I'm working on it," said Evan, and her pants were off a millisecond later, leaving her in just the bikini bottoms.

She bit her lip. "I'm just...I'm not perfect, you know."

Dean feigned shock. "You aren't? That's nonsense." He cupped her breast, though his gaze never left hers. "You have the most amazing boobs."

"So romantic," she teased.

"Your thighs are like the loveliest alabaster," said Evan, running his hand down one.

Tamsyn giggled despite her nervousness, and it eased her tension. When Dean bent to kiss her, she offered her mouth eagerly, moaning into his a second later when Evan's finger breached the side of her bikini to stroke her moist curls.

Her hand seemed to have a mind of its own, and she sought out Dean's erection as he deepened their kiss. His flesh was smooth and hard, waiting for the first touch of her fingers as she gently explored him. Tamsyn wrapped her hand around his shaft and stroked him softly.

Evan continued touching her in a way that was perfection, as though he knew better than she did what her body needed to come alive. Dean's kisses were stealing her ability to think logically as surely as the fire his twin stoked between her thighs, leaving her a writhing, heated mess as she kissed and stroked with abandon.

At some point, their touches turned into one in her mind. She was aware of them as distinct individuals, of course, but they moved together like a unit. Dean and Evan seemed to know when to shift in concert, or when to tease her with contrasting sensations. It was unlike anything she'd ever experienced, and the orgasm they coaxed from her with just kissing and caressing was more powerful than even her most intense previous encounter with anyone else.

While she trembled under the force of her climax, Dean found release before collapsing onto the deck beside her. He put his head on her shoulder and kissed her skin tenderly a couple of times. Even with Dean beside her, it wasn't awkward to reach for Evan's cock and bring him pleasure as he had given her.

Afterward, the three of them lay together on the gently rocking boat, heartbeats slowing and breathing growing less raspy.

"That was amazing," she whispered, unable to believe how much she had enjoyed what could technically be considered only mild foreplay. If they could leave her this shattered with petting, how was she going to survive making love with them? It was a delicious prospect, and she knew she was ready for the next step.

"I just realized this deck is really fucking uncomfortable," said Dean, wincing as he stretched and sat up.

"Nah, you're just an old man," said Evan, sitting up as well.

"I prefer the term mature," said Dean. "You'll understand when you reach my age."

Tamsyn shook her head. "He's ten minutes younger than you."

"It's made all the difference."

"Yep. I'm still the young and fun one." Evan winked.

She eyed them both with appreciation as they each grasped one of her hands and eased her into a sitting position. "I'd say you're both fun, Evan." Licking her lips, she said, "I'm suddenly eager to find out just how much fun the two of you are when you tackle a task together."

Dean and Evan shared a look. "We don't want to rush you."

"There's no reason to hurry things along," added Dean.

Tamsyn frowned. "Do you two not want to...have sex with me yet?"

They shared another look before both squeezing her hand. "We do."

"Of course we do." Evan brushed his lips against her fingers when he lifted her hand to his mouth.

"We just want to make sure the foundation is in place first." Dean tucked a strand of dark hair behind her ear. "This is something special, love, and we want you to know that. Slow and steady is just fine."

She tilted her head slightly. "You're making sure I feel comfortable with how things progress, right?" At their nods, she smiled slightly. "I am very comfortable with the path we're treading, and I would like to make love with you...both of you...sooner rather than later."

"Oh." Dean swallowed audibly.

"Is that something you would like?" Feeling more confident now that she saw their eagerness, she reached for her cover-up and slipped it on, sans bikini top.

"More than anything," said Evan in a thick voice.

"How soon do you think you can get us home?" she asked with a teasing grin. The word resonated in her mind, feeling right, and she realized she felt more at home in their apartment than she ever had at her parents' stuffy Victorian. Like the Gaines' family home, it was the people who lived there who made her feel welcome. More than that, they were starting to feel like an essential part of her, the pieces she hadn't recognized as missing until now.

"Ready to set some speed records, Ev?" asked Dean with a big grin.

"Of course, there is a bed below-deck." She looked up at them flirtatiously through her lashes.

The twins groaned, but shook their heads in unison. "Our first time isn't going to be on a tiny queen-size bed," said Dean.

She licked her lips. "Are you sure? A queen isn't that small. It might be...cozy."

Evan groaned, but seemed to find enough resolve to stand up. "You're a teasing vixen, and we're going to make you pay for that later, Tamsyn."

"Promises, promises," she said with a laugh, feeling free and lighthearted. It seemed easy and entirely possible to be with the twins in all ways.

For the first time since she had agreed to start dating them, she could really envision a future where their nontraditional relationship worked. A future with kids and family around them, where they lived without being embarrassed by their arrangement—where she was too happy with her men to spare consideration for others' disapproval. For a girl raised in such a repressive environment and used to having to consider public opinion before making any decisions, it was a heady thought.

Chapter Five

BY THE TIME THEY DOCKED in Seattle and took the coupe back to the apartment, Tamsyn was dying with impatience to reach the large bed in the spacious bedroom where she had been sleeping. Her mind was full of scenarios and delightful possibilities that made her body burn with desire and seduced her senses.

She blamed that pre-sex anticipation for blinding her to Will's presence until they had almost reached the front door. The sight of her former fiancé standing at his brothers' apartment entrance was like a dunk in the icy waters of the Strait. All her previous euphoria fled, and her cheeks bloomed with color as she remembered the erotic encounter she'd just had with the twins a few hours before. Was it obvious what she had been doing?

Self-consciously, she crossed her arms over her breasts, remembering for the first time all afternoon that she hadn't bothered to put on her bikini top again when she had redressed on the yacht.

He looked embarrassed, and his ears were tinged with a hint of red at the tips, just as they always were when he blushed. Will didn't look at his brothers, and his gaze didn't waver from Tamsyn's. "Hi."

She frowned at him, torn between ignoring him, screaming at him, and allowing the sweetly awkward way he scuffed the toe of his shoe to soften her. A quick glance at Evan and Dean revealed their obvious hostility toward their brother, and she winced. The last thing she'd want was for their relationship with Will to suffer because of her.

Biting her lip, she stood frozen with indecision. Finally, she asked, "What are you doing here?"

"Can we talk? Please?" He gave her a pleading look, one that never failed to melt her irritation.

This time, she was still annoyed with him, but she couldn't refuse, could she? They had been on the verge of marrying just a few days before, so she should at least talk to him. Right? Another glance at the twins showed they probably wouldn't have agreed with her, but neither one said anything or tried to stop her when she nodded. "Okay."

"Let's go get coffee." He held out his hand.

Hesitantly, she took it, letting her ex-fiancé lead her from the twins. When she looked back at the two men, they stared at her impassively, but with a resigned set to their shoulders that suggested they believed they had already lost her.

Chapter Six

WILL CHOSE COFFEE SHOP closest to Dean and Evan's apartment, ordering Tamsyn a cinnamon vanilla latte without having to ask her preference. Before he'd shocked her with news of the canceled wedding, she would have considered it another sign of his devotion. Now, she couldn't help wondering if he knew his mystery woman's coffee preferences as well as he knew hers. "Why have you brought me here, Will?"

"I owe you a huge apology, love," said Will, the tips of his ears bright red in his embarrassment.

Tamsyn scoffed. "You owe me more than that for what you've done to me." She stirred her coffee in a desultory fashion, unwilling to meet his gaze. It wasn't that she feared crumbling before him so much as she was enjoying his discomfort.

He hung his head like a chastened child. "I made a terrible mistake, Tamsyn. I only hope you can forgive me for what I've done."

She arched a skeptical brow. "How do I know you won't change your mind again? I mean what led to your epiphany? What did you suddenly decide I was the one you wanted instead of the woman you cheated on me with?"

Will looked miserable. "I realized we didn't want the same things. When I started discussing our future, Sharti made it clear we don't have one. She has an arranged marriage waiting for her in India, and she is not willing to jeopardize that."

Aghast, Tamsyn stared at him in disbelief. "I see," she said calmly. "You decided since you couldn't have Sharti, you would settle for me. Is that right?" What in the world was she doing here, sitting across from her ex-fiancé? Right now, she could have been in that huge bed with Dean and Evan.

Will's face flamed scarlet. "That's not what I meant. You have to know that's not what I meant."

She sniffed softly. "If you say so."

He reached across the table to lift her limp hand into his. "Please believe me, Tamsyn. When I had a chance to think about it, I knew I'd made a horrible mistake. The relationship with Sharti was exciting and new. I let the sex blind me to the fact she and I weren't anything real or serious." He traced his thumb over the back of her hand. "Not like you and me. We're real."

"Just not fun or sexy." She withdrew her hand despite his brief resistance, using it to grasp her coffee. "I've been doing some thinking too, Will, and I realized you were right to call things off."

He blinked. "What? No, I wasn't. I was a blind, selfish fool."

She inclined her head, certainly not willing to placate him with false assurances that he hadn't been. "I was angry and humiliated, but it also made me realize I wasn't exactly devastated by losing you. I was more upset about having to face everyone and have them know I'd done something wrong, or there was something lacking in me."

He frowned. "You're fine just as you are."

Damned by faint praise. Tamsyn almost grinned as she remembered the sweet compliments Dean and Evan had bestowed upon her. They were sometimes extravagant or comical, but she didn't doubt their sincerity. "I know that now, but I spent some agonizing days worrying about how I could fix me before I realized you were the problem."

Will scowled. "It wasn't all me, Tamsyn. I wouldn't have looked at Sharti if—" He broke off abruptly. "Look, this isn't productive. Can we please move forward?"

A thrill of amusement shot through her, and she was a bit surprised by how much joy she was taking from watching her ex squirm. "No, please finish your thought. You wouldn't have looked if what? I was skinnier? More adventurous in bed?"

He lifted a shoulder. "Things are pretty dull in that area, but I've realized I'd rather have predictable than exciting. I know you'll always be there. Predictable is good."

Tamsyn let out a hearty laugh. "Will, you will always be my friend, I think, but you're such a gigantic ass that I'm relieved I discovered it before we got married."

He took a deep breath, seeming to be trying to control his temper. "I know you're still hurt and angry, but could we please focus on the future? The bedroom stuff doesn't matter."

"But it does." Tamsyn took another sip of her coffee. "We are boring together, Will, but *I'm* not boring. I've discovered a whole new side to myself, and it's time to embrace it. I think you should do whatever makes you happy, as long as you revise that plan not to include me."

He scowled. "Stop being so childish, Tamsyn. You're not going to do better than me."

Her eyes widened. "Wow."

His ears turned red. "I just meant that you and I are great together. It can't get better."

"Yeah, that's exactly what you meant." She pushed away her cup and slid back her chair. "The thing is, without any effort, I could find something twice as good as what we had." With a giggle, she stood up. "No, make that about a thousand times better."

He frowned. "Are you trying to claim you're seeing someone else?"

"Um hmm."

Will's face took on a petulant look. "Were you cheating on me?"

She arched a brow. "I don't think you have the right to ask me that, but no, I wasn't. I found out how they felt after you and I had split."

"They?" His eyes narrowed. "Are you slutting around with two men?"

"Oh, yes, I am." Smoothing down her swimsuit cover-up, ensuring her nipples were prominent, she gave him one last look. "If you'll excuse me, I'm going to go embrace my harlotude now, Will."

His mouth gaped open as she turned from him. He called her name, but she didn't pause or look back. Instead, she focused on her destination. Will was behind her, and in the past, while Evan and Dean were firmly in front of her. They were her future if they still wanted her.

Chapter Seven

WHEN SHE RETURNED TO their apartment, the door was ajar. Hesitantly, she stepped inside, just a bit frightened of their reception. What if they didn't want her anymore? After all, she had abandoned them to go with Will. At the time, it had seemed like she owed him a chance to explain, but that was silly. She prayed she hadn't hurt the two men with whom she was falling in love in her attempt to be fair to the man she hadn't really loved the way she should have to marry him.

"Dean? Evan?" she called their names softly, entering the living room to find them sprawled out on each of the two long sofas, both looking morose. "Hey," she said softly.

"Did you come back for your things?" asked Dean, sounding neutral about the whole idea. The flash in his copper eyes betrayed his pain at the idea.

She shook her head.

"Going to leave them and let your fiancé buy you new ones?" asked Evan, not quite as successful at maintaining neutrality.

Tamsyn shook her head again. "No, I'd like to keep my things where I left them."

"We're not running a storage service," said Evan.

She nodded, forcing back a smile. "I know. I plan to be here to use them, if you don't mind me staying a while longer?"

Evan sat up, eyeing her for a second. "How long is a while?"

Tamsyn tipped her head. "I know we'll need to take it one day at a time, but I'm hoping for at least sixty or seventy years?"

"What about Will?" asked Dean.

She lifted a shoulder. "It's your apartment, but I'd prefer he not stay here."

Evan whooped as he bounded to his feet. A second later, his brother was beside him, and they were closing in on her fast. Instead of being fearful, she shivered with anticipation. "I'm sorry I left with him."

"I suppose you owed it to him," said Dean, though he didn't seem to believe it.

She shook her head. "No, I didn't owe him anything." A giggle escaped her. "Remind me to recount his not-so-suave verbal gymnastics." Evan's arm went around her waist, and Dean stood on her other side, cradling the back of her head with his hand. "Some other time, when you need a laugh."

Dean's lips on hers swallowed the last word, and she softened hers, molding to him and deepening the kiss. Evan's hands made short work of her swimsuit cover-up, and she was soon between them in just capris and bikini bottoms. Tamsyn surrendered to them as they steered her toward the bedroom, alternating kisses between each of her soon-to-be lovers.

Once inside the room, they stopped near the bed. After shedding the rest of her clothes, she stepped back from them to allow the men to undress, her appreciative gaze running over their solid forms. Their large erections jutted frontward as though reaching for her, and she let her instincts guide her.

Reaching forward, she grasped one in each hand, gently pulling the men closer. "This is so much more than I ever thought I'd have," she confessed, letting her dark hair obscure her face to hide the sheen of tears in her eyes. The last thing they would want was for her to burst into tears in the middle of sex. Even happy tears might kill the mood, and she wouldn't risk that.

Evan nudged her head up gently, leaning forward to lick away the single teardrop escaping her rapidly blinking eyes. "You're more than we ever thought we'd have. You're everything to us, Tamsyn."

Dean stepped behind her, his shaft pressing into the small of her back as he cupped her shoulders. "We've known for a while that you were the one for us, but we don't want to frighten you, so there's no rush. You can stop at any time."

She chuckled, though it was more of a breathy, broken sound when Evan bent to take her nipple into his mouth. "I think stopping would kill me, dears."

Evan said something around her nipple. She couldn't make out the words but figured he was agreeing with her. Her hands had fallen to her sides when they had moved position, but now she lifted them, stretching one behind her to tangle in Dean's hair as he nibbled her neck, while grasping Evan's hair with the other.

Together, they moved toward the bed, and she lay down first with both of them on either side of her. It felt so right to be between them. Her mouth sought Evan's in a deep kiss as Dean slid farther down the bed, lifting one of her legs to settle his head between them.

She moaned with anticipation, already wet with need before his mouth even touched her sensitive core. Tamsyn arched to meet him, and his tongue slipped inside her, stroking and teasing her.

Evan deepened the kiss, and his erection brushed her hand. She grasped it, but wasn't content just to touch him this time. With a ragged exhalation, she turned her hed from his kiss while pulling lightly upward, to show him what she wanted.

"I'm going to love you forever," he said with a groan as he shifted positions to bring his shaft to her mouth.

Tamsyn took him inside, enjoying his moans of passion that echoed the ones escaping her from Dean's ministrations. As her orgasm approached, she cried out around Evan, but didn't stop her attentions.

Almost as soon as she had come, Dean was moving positions, this time kneeling between her legs. Vaguely, she heard the tear of foil, and then he was entering her. Slowly and gently, making her whimper with need and the pleasure of being filled so deeply.

Evan stiffened, his hips jutting forward as he twitched inside her mouth. His warm seed coated her tongue, and she drank greedily until he pulled away with a moan, clearly too sensitive to allow her to continue.

Dean thrust in and out of her in a slow and steady pace as Evan returned his attention to her breasts, sometimes pausing to kiss her mouth before returning to a taut pink bud. A warm tickling sensation spread out from her womb, making her lower body clench. Another release swept over her as Dean thrust deeply inside her, the heat of his orgasm warm through the condom.

Seamlessly, like a machine, the men soon changed places, and she locked gazes with Evan as he slid carefully into her folds. The love in his eyes warmed her, and she saw the same expression on Dean's face when she looked at him before he bent to kiss her. As Evan made love to her, and she took Dean into her mouth, she knew she had made the right decision.

Chapter Eight

THE EVENTS HALL WAS packed, and Tamsyn couldn't help wondering cynically how many of the attendees had accepted just to see the oddity about to play out before them. With a shrug, she decided she didn't care as she turned back to her mother, who stood waiting for her. The important people would be there to celebrate her union with Dean and Evan, and gossipmongers could...well, they could find interesting ways to amuse themselves with their own genitals.

"Tamsyn, come here. You still need to be laced in."

She smothered a groan as she went to stand with her back to her mother. That Diane was here at all was a major miracle, and one she owed mainly to her father. Despite her mother's conviction that she could make her husband turn against Tamsyn, Rudolph had proven to be made of sterner stuff.

It had been a surprise to learn her father was quietly proud of her, and while not a demonstrative or emotional man, he did love her. She didn't doubt that any longer, having borne witness to the times he had stood firm with Diane when she had tried to abandon the wedding planning or cut off Tamsyn for the newest outrage.

Still, she would have expected Flora to be in the brides' room with her, having expected her mother to take ill or something at the last moment. She assumed Diane had summoned the fortitude to endure her role so she didn't have to live with the gossip of having been supplanted by *that woman*. After all, if she played the martyr of having selflessly endured her daughter's shameful behavior, it would go over well with her social set.

"Geez, Mother, you aren't going to get me down a size with that thing." The wedding dress had been a concession to tradition and her mother, and it included a laced-up corset. While striking, it was darned uncomfortable, and she was already looking forward to having Dean and Evan strip it off her later that evening—for more than one reason.

With some grunting and huffing on both their parts, her mother finally stood back, apparently satisfied she had squished her daughter's organs to the limit. Surprisingly, her purple-blue eyes had a sheen of moisture. "You look lovely, Tamsyn."

"Um, thanks." She cleared her throat, unexpectedly assaulted by the lump of moisture that rose from her mother's rare display of emotion.

"I suppose it's time." She spoke with a small sigh, as though regretting that it was at last the hour at which to publicly subject herself to the travesty about to take place.

Feeling more amused than annoyed with her mother, Tamsyn leaned forward to press a kiss to her cool cheek. "Thank you for being here, Mother."

Another surprise waited when Diane clutched her arm lightly. "I wouldn't miss your w...wedding, dear."

Her eyes widened at the use of the word that her mother had carefully avoided over the past few months. It was always the "event" or the "thing," but never ceremony, celebration, or wedding.

Her mother sighed. "I owe you an apology for my earlier behavior. I won't pretend to approve of this unorthodox...thing you're doing here, but you are my daughter, and I love you. That won't ever change."

Tamsyn blinked, refusing to shed tears and ruin her makeup. "I love you too, Mom." Only the knowledge that her mother would squirm with discomfort kept her from throwing her arms around the other woman for a big hug.

After a moment of blinking and throat clearing, Diane handed her a bouquet of orchids, dyed a vibrant orange. She clutched the bouquet and walked out with her mother.

In the hall, her bridesmaids waited in a procession of orange, along with her maid-of-honor. Jaely smiled at her before bending down to whisper to Lacey to stand in front of her. When the little girl was positioned correctly, Tamsyn knelt down to whisper, "Are you ready to be my flower girl?"

"I been ready for months and months," said Lacey with a little huff at having been denied her first opportunity. She didn't seem to notice or care that the groom had changed, and she had been thrilled to get two pretty dresses in the span of a few months.

Her bright orange dress was a perfect match for the women of the wedding party and coordinated with her father's bowtie and waistcoat. When she had chosen themes and colors for this wedding, Tamsyn had ignored tradition as much as possible. She hadn't fussed over choosing between smoke or snow white anything. Instead, she'd chosen a bright color that matched her joy in the union.

The attendant opened the double doors, and she sat off down the aisle, surrounded by friends and family. Her gaze didn't waver from the two men waiting for her, and she grinned when she saw their surprise. Instead of the orange waistcoat and bowtie like her father and the ring-bearer wore, they had gone for all-orange tuxes with white bowties.

The color clashed horribly with their hair, but the sight was so happy that she burst into laughter. As she neared them, she couldn't help calling out, "I love you two so much."

"That part comes later," said Diane, but with a small wink that softened any hint of rebuke.

With another small laugh, Tamsyn released her father's arm and took one of each of the men's she was about to marry. Of course they couldn't all legally marry, so they had made the choice to just celebrate their union with a private ceremony and not worry about the legal side of marriage, like licenses.

The celebrant greeted them warmly before addressing the guests to welcome them to the union. The words were almost identical to a traditional marriage ceremony, and she repeated her lines without hesitation. Soon, their rings nestled on her finger, and she slid a platinum band on each of their hands.

When they kissed her, first Evan and then Dean, she heard a whisper of conversation behind her, but didn't let it distract her. The people in attendance would have to get used to the sight of her being affectionate with her husbands, because she wasn't going to let the world dictate how she showed her love.

Epilogue

"HEY, THERE'S A CARD here from Will," said Evan as he dumped the pile of mail onto the coffee table and came to sit beside Tamsyn. Dean was on her other side, feeding her ice cream.

"Hmm, I wonder what he's up to?" asked his brother. "We haven't seen him since he disappeared before our wedding."

Tamsyn shrugged, scooting sideways to stretch her legs across Evan's lap. She wiggled her toes to let him know what she wanted. His foot rubs were to die for, and she was unashamedly spoiled by them.

"Hang on, love." He slit the envelope with one finger in a move that should have left a long paper cut, but he made seem effortless. A white card slipped out, and he barked a laugh a moment later. "I'll be damned."

"What is it?" asked Dean as he scooped another spoon of ice cream into her mouth.

"I guess our little bro has been in India. Apparently, he was inspired by us to fight for true love."

Tamsyn snorted.

"No, that's what the little handwritten note says." Evan's eyes twinkled. "He must have gotten Sharti to change her mind, because we're all invited to his wedding in two months."

"Where?" asked Dean, shooting a glance downward.

"New Delhi."

Tamsyn sighed. "I guess we can't make it." She patted her tummy, silently thankful she would be spared seeing Will marry his perfect woman. Not that she harbored any emotions for him any longer, but it could still be quite awkward. The twins gave her a perfect excuse to avoid it. "I'll be in the third trimester by then, but I suppose you guys could go."

"Never," said Evan.

"Absolutely not." Dean put a hand on her belly.

Evan did the same a moment later, and the girls obliged by kicking their daddies' hands. "We aren't leaving you or them."

"We'll have to send a huge gift though," said Dean.

"Why's that?" asked Tamsyn, suddenly remembering Will hadn't sent them a present. She hadn't expected him to, and she didn't care, but it made her wonder why his brother felt so moved to be generous.

"Oh, because if he hadn't been such a moron, we wouldn't have you with us right now," said Evan, as though it was the most obvious answer in the world. "We would have sent you a huge thank you sooner—"

"If we'd known where he was," finished Dean.

She laughed and shook her head. "I think Will got just what he deserved, and I know I certainly did." Slowly, she leaned forward, knowing they would insist on helping her up from the couch in about two seconds. "Now, take me to bed."

"You need a nap?" asked Evan casually.

"Hmm...eventually." She gave them a wink.

They traded looks and hustled her to her feet. It never failed to amuse or amaze her how quickly they could move when they worked together.

If you enjoyed this story and would like to receive notifications of new releases or access bonus chapters for your favorite books, please join my Mailing List[1]. You'll also receive six books just for joining. If you prefer to receive notifications for just one, or a few, of my pen names, you'll have the option to select which lists to subscribe to at signup.

And keep reading for an excerpt of another Kit Kyndall title.

---

1. http://kittunstall.com/newsletter/

Bonus Excerpt

Model Behavior

WHEN CURVY EMMA MODELS for a family friend shooting pictures for romance novel covers, she isn't expecting there to be a second model. Cody is hot enough to melt her new panties, but that makes it harder to pose intimately with him and pretend she isn't attracted. It doesn't take long to realize the attraction is mutual, and their steamy photography session leads to a night of intense passion that can't be anything else. They're too different for it to be more than one night. Aren't they?

A standalone story with no cliffhangers.

Emma bit back a nervous giggle as she let herself into Mona's photography studio. She'd been here a few times before and each time the décor was different, though the white wall and lights remained static. Today, she was a bit unnerved to find a bedroom scene in the main studio when she walked past reception to find her mother's best friend.

"Mona?" she called hesitantly.

"In here, dear."

Following the sound of her voice, she entered a changing area off the side of the studio. Her mother's petite friend was in the process of hanging something. Thin and energetic, with black hair shorn close to her head, Mona always reminded her of a crow darting around. "Hey." She stood awkwardly, not sure what to expect.

Emma had never seen herself as model material. She knew she was pretty, having heard she had "such a pretty face" often enough, and she was tall, but she wasn't a model. Not that she had ever dreamed of being a supermodel, but her ample curves would have killed that dream if she had.

Apparently not though, according to Mona. Curvy models were in demand, especially for books featuring curvy heroines. Having read more than her share of Mina Carter and other curvy authors, Emma could appreciate the desire to have a cover model match the heroine's description.

It hadn't been that motivating her to give in to Mona's pleading for her to pose for some pictures, as much as she liked the idea of having a woman of size on a romance book cover. Simply, it had been great affection for the other woman, who was her aunt in all ways but blood.

Also, she had to admit the idea of being transformed into a curvy goddess for a day appealed to her. It would be a fun way to see how the other half lived, or something like that. What girl didn't secretly dream of being photographed and admired? Despite her lack of supermodel ambitions, she couldn't pretend the fantasy didn't appeal.

After spending ten minutes applying a light layer of makeup, Mona nodded. "Right, we have a busy day ahead of us, dear. If you could please put on this black nightie, we'll start with those shots." She walked over to the rack to lift a hanger holding a garment of gauzy black decorated with lace panels and a rhinestone heart at the bustline.

Emma eyed it doubtfully. "Um, you want me to wear that, Mona?"

Mona shook the hanger gently. "Yes, and do hurry. I have a lot of ground to cover today."

She bit her lip. "Don't you think it's a bit revealing?"

The smaller woman rolled her eyes. "Of course it is, dear. We want to meet a wide range of needs. Some of your images might end up on erotic novels."

Her heart jumped at the thought. "You mean guys might masturbate to my picture?" She didn't know whether to be repulsed or flattered.

Mona laughed. "Perhaps, my dear, but it's far more likely to be women. They're the main readers of erotica."

Emma's eyes widened. "Really?" Reluctantly, she reached out for the nightie. "Well, okay." It was a little strange, but she'd already clarified with Mona that there would be no nudity when she had signed the model release last week.

As soon as Mona left, she shed the simple blue jeans and white shirt she'd been instructed to wear, folding them neatly before slipping on the nightie.

It molded to her curves while somehow fluttering around them. The black was a beautiful contrast to her porcelain skin and bright auburn hair. Unfortunately, the bra underneath ruined the effect, and she didn't have to ask to know Mona would want her to remove it.

With a bit of lingerie gymnastics, she took off the bra without having to remove the nightie. Then, taking a deep breath, she forced herself to step out of the dressing room and into the studio.

"Lovely," said Mona, but in a brisk way that felt impersonal. "Let's get started."

Emma walked over to stand in front of the white wall, doing her best to comply with her honorary aunt's instructions. She soon discovered that while modeling left one feeling sexy and desired, it was also precise and kind of exhausting. It was a relief when Mona finally called a halt forty minutes later after taking what seemed to be an infinite number of pictures.

"Great job, dear. Now please return to the dressing room and slip on the white shirt and jeans you wore in."

Emma nodded, heading that direction. She froze when she heard her name. "Yes, Mona?"

"No bra this time, dear."

With a tight nod, she returned to the dressing room. The nightie slid off easily, and she was soon redressed in her street clothes sans bra. Gulping quietly, she stared at her generous breasts through the thin white halter shirt. The ribbing did nothing to hide the dusky pinkness of her areolas or shield the taut buds of her nipples. The shirt was actually sexier than the nightie somehow.

Feeling a bit daunted, Emma stepped out of the dressing room. Shaking out her hair, she wasn't paying attention. "Okay, Mona, let's get this over with before my boobs explode out of this—uh." She collided with a solid male presence that made her head snap up.

Even though she was tall, he was taller. Gorgeous too, with a nice tan, sparkling blue eyes, and thick, black curls topping his head. Her fingers itched to stroke them, and she balled her hand into a fist to curb the impulse. "Oh, sorry. I didn't expect anyone else." Her face bloomed with color as she silently added she wouldn't have been discussing her boobs if she had.

He grinned, his eyes dipping very briefly to her cleavage before returning to meet her hazel gaze. "No problem."

"Emma, darling, this is Cody Lemott. Cody, this is Emma Baylor."

Emma took his hand, shaking firmly, while shooting Mona a puzzled look. "What's he doing here, Mona?"

"He's the other model, dear."

Emma blinked. "Uh, what?"

Mona gave her a puzzled look with her sharp, dark eyes. "We're doing romance covers here, dear, so readers are going to expect to see a couple."

"Oh." Oh god, why hadn't she realized that? Why hadn't she asked Mona about the possibility? Emma was reasonably secure with her curves, having had twenty years to get used to the state of her body, but the idea of modeling in couples' poses with the hot guy beside her left her stomach churning with dread.

"Cody's ready. I did his makeup while you changed."

Emma nodded, eyes widening with relief that at least he hadn't come in while she was still wearing that nightie. As her mother liked to say, it could always be worse.

Somehow, she forced her feet to move as she walked behind Cody back to the space in front of the lights. Her gaze rested on the taut curve of his buttocks in the dark blue jeans, and she had to make herself look away. The bed was off to the side of the place Mona was currently highlighting with the studio lights, and her stomach dipped again with the idea of having to pose with him on that.

No way. Mona wouldn't go that far, and she wouldn't allow it if her mother's friend tried to persuade her. They'd have a couple of embracing pictures, and then Emma could clear out and let Mona do a one-on-one shoot with Cody.

"All right, dears, we're not robots. Stand loosely and relax."

Emma focused on her instructions, taking a deep breath that gradually unclenched her muscles.

"Now lean back against him, Emma. Put your head on his chest."

Cautiously, she eased into the directed position, letting her head barely touch his chest. This was so awkward. She hadn't done a lot of touching with the opposite sex, and the impersonal nature of this made it even stranger when it should have provided a buffer.

"Relax, Emma. Take a deep breath and rest against him."

"I won't bite," said Cody in a low whisper, and his reassuring tone helped her relax. "Unless you ask me to," he added in a teasing tone.

She stiffened again, but forced herself to sink against the firmly muscled chest and abdomen behind her.

"Good. Cody, put your hand on her hip." Mona took a couple of pictures before issuing new instructions. "Now wrap your arm around her waist, hand on her tummy."

Emma fought really hard not to jump like a skittish kitten when he followed the photographer's instructions. Her fight got harder a second later.

"Now splay your hand out wide, Cody, fingers pointing downward. You're reaching for her pussy."

"Mona!" Emma didn't know if she was more shocked by the casual vulgarity or the suggestion—or even how quickly Cody obeyed her. She trembled slightly when his hand spread across her abdomen, the tip of his middle finger just a few inches above her mound.

"Don't be such a prude, dear," said Mona in a dismissive way.

She didn't consider her reaction prudish, but she resisted the urge to snap at Mona. Instead, she forced herself to pretend to be calm and stand in what she hoped was a passably relaxed way.

"Very good."

It seemed like it took Mona ten years to take enough pictures before she was satisfied. During the entire process, Emma endured the touch of the stranger.

Okay, endured was a strong word. More like withstood her own need to cuddle closer and let his hand drift lower. It was a ridiculous reaction, and she reminded herself this was strictly business. Cody was behaving like a professional, and she needed to do the same despite her amateur model status.

"Excellent. Emma, turn toward Cody. Wrap your hands in his T-shirt, and pull it up his chest."

Still focused on trying to be professional, she did as Mona told her, bunching the cotton around her hand in what seemed an awkward way. Cody's indrawn breath had her freezing, and she looked up at him. "Am I hurting you?" She tried not to move her lips when she asked, in case Mona was actively photographing them.

"Killing me," he said softly.

She frowned, trying to decide what could be bothering him.

"Now lean in closer, Emma. I want your torsos pressed together. You're urgent for each other."

With a small sigh, she complied before issuing her own gasp as their bodies met. The hard point of his erection against her hip was a shock. Perhaps he wasn't as professional as he had seemed.

"Hold that pose."

Emma stared up at him, trying to keep her expression neutral even in the face of his obvious embarrassment tinged with amusement. "Hurry up, Mona," she said through mostly closed lips.

"There's no need to rush." Cody bent his head to bring their mouths just a few inches apart. "I'm having a wonderful time."

Her eyes widened even as she heard Mona's praise.

"Excellent, Cody. Hold that, and now kiss."

She remained frozen when his lips touched hers, unable to respond due to shock. Could it be this guy really found her attractive, or was he just a good actor?

"He's not your brother, dear. Try to relax and summon some enthusiasm. Put your arms around his neck and hold on. Yes, like that." Mona sounded pleased as her camera clicked. "Now, lips touching again."

It was strange to press her lips to his. They remained still, not really kissing, but giving the appearance of it. It was more awkward than her first kiss, when she hadn't known what to do with her hands or how to tilt her head to avoid hitting Kyle Whitley's nose.

"Great. Now for something else."

Emma started to step back, gasping silently when Cody's tongue flicked over the seam of her lips before he stepped back to await further instructions. She barely resisted the urge to let her own tongue follow the same path as she looked away, confused by his actions.

And turned on. She couldn't deny her pulse was suddenly pounding in her ears, and that her nipples had gotten harder.

"Okay, shirts off, lovelies."

Emma stared at her mother's friend as she saw Cody instantly comply, pulling off his shirt as though it was no big deal. With a body like that, it probably wasn't. Lord, she wanted to touch his skin to see if it was soft over the hard muscles.

"*Tout de suite*, Emma," barked Mona.

She jumped, but still didn't pull up her tank top. "You said no nudity, Mona."

Available at your preferred ebook vendor or directly on the author's website[1].

---

1. http://kittunstall.com/downloads/mb/

Author Bio

Kit Kyndall is the pen name *USA Today* bestselling author Kit Tunstall uses when writing steamy, erotic contemporary romances. It's simply a way to separate the myriad types of stories she writes so readers know what to expect with each "author."

KIT TUNSTALL LIVES in Idaho with her husband and two sons. She enjoys writing several genres and subgenres, but almost everything she writes has a strong romantic element. A fan of post-apocalyptic, zombie, and dystopian books, she prefers to read or view such stories from the comfort of her living room and never, ever in person.

[Website](1)

---

1. http://www.kittunstall.com

Did you love *Double Delights*? Then you should read *Playing His Game*[2] by Kit Kyndall!

Maya will do anything for her fiancé, Bobby. Roarke is willing to do anything to have Maya, and he blackmails her into a game of seduction. She expects him to be selfish and demanding, so his tender wooing is a surprise. As Roarke breaks down her walls and opens her eyes to the flaws in her relationship with Bobby, she wonders if there will be a winner in their game, or if they're both playing for keeps.

This is a complete standalone novel with no cliffhangers.

---

2. https://books2read.com/u/3nRV53

3. https://books2read.com/u/3nRV53

Also by Kit Kyndall

Kingwood Prep
Catching His Eye

Protectors
Safe Harbor
Hart & Soal

Pure Escapes
Ablaze
Out Of Bounds
Guarded
Succumb
Taking
Proposition
I'm No Saint Nick

Sage Valley
Reunion

A Second Chance

Seen
Catching His Eye, Part 1
Catching His Eye, Pt. 2
Catching His Eye, Pt. 3

SpicyShorts
Pawn
Two Cowboys for Cady
Ebony Enigma
Wrong Groom
Model Behavior
Biology Lessons
Mai Tais on the Beach
All Grown Up
SpicyShorts Bundle

Sweet Escapes
Falling For A Firefighter
Worth Waiting

Well...
Well-Seasoned